**She should pull away and ask him to take her home.**

So why was she doing nothing to stop him when he ran the flat of his hand down over one breast and then back again?

Because she couldn't, that was why.

Two flares of colour ran along each aristocratic cheekbone, and at that moment Darian looked pure Marabanese, with all the accompanying pride and arrogance of that desert ancestry.

Yet his hard mouth had been softened by her kisses, so that for one second he looked unexpectedly vulnerable. It was like having a curtain twitched and seeing behind it a glimpse of a man that you dared not dream existed. A man with softness beneath the hard, polished exterior, making him utterly irresistible. And with something approaching shock Lara realised that she wanted him now, no matter what the consequences.

Born in West London, **Sharon Kendrick** now lives in the beautiful city of Winchester, and can hear the bells of the Cathedral ringing out while she works. She has had zillions of jobs, which include photographer, nurse, waitress and demonstrator of ironing board covers. She drove an ambulance in Australia and appeared on television in Teheran, but writing is the only job she's had which feels just right. Her passions are many and varied, but include music, films, books, cooking, gazing at the sky and drifting off in daydreams while she works out passionate new love-stories!

**Recent titles by the same author:**

THE ITALIAN'S LOVE-CHILD
THE GREEK'S SECRET PASSION
BACK IN THE BOSS'S BED

# THE DESERT PRINCE'S MISTRESS

BY

SHARON KENDRICK

MILLS & BOON®

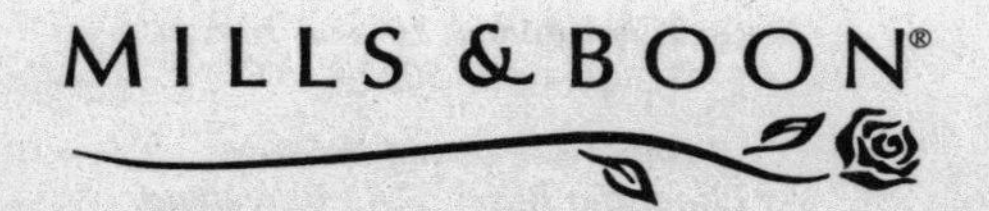

To Sarah and David Nicholson,
Wilf and Hubie,
who always provide a place
of chaos and fun in Winchester!



*First published in Great Britain 2004*
*Harlequin Mills & Boon Limited,*
*Eton House, 18-24 Paradise Road, Richmond, Surrey TW9 1SR*



ISBN 0 263 83721 1

*Set in Times Roman 10½ on 11½ pt.*
*01-0304-50259*

*Printed and bound in Spain*
*by Litografia Rosés, S.A., Barcelona*

# CHAPTER ONE

IN HER hands she held dynamite.

Not real dynamite but something equally explosive, and Lara's fingers trembled as she looked down at the letter.

Above her head, the magnificent and ornate chandeliers of the Maraban Embassy threw glittering diamonds of light down onto the sheet of paper, and Lara stared at it, knowing that this letter held information which could change the lives of so many.

If it was true.

Lara swallowed, wondering if she should have opened it in the first place—but wasn't that part of her job, as demanded by her temporary role as secretary, to open the post? A job which up until about ten minutes ago had seemed as perfect as a fill-in job could possibly be. Her recent appointment had been a blessing for the Embassy, because their usual employee was off sick, and a blessing for her, too—since work hadn't exactly been thick on the ground recently. As a model and actress she had been 'resting' so much that lately she'd wondered why she even bothered getting out of bed in the morning.

The letter was written in a slightly wavery style, though whether that was due to the age of its author or to the emotional impact of the contents, Lara didn't know. The letter was also dated over two years ago, but somebody had obviously only recently posted it for it to have arrived just this morning.

Could it be a forgery? She supposed it could.

She read it again, slowly, taking in each incredible word.

To whom it may concern.

I wish to inform you that my son, Darian Wildman, is the progeny of the late Sheikh Makim, Monarch of Maraban. The Sheikh was unaware that he had a child outside wedlock, and indeed Darian himself has no idea of the identity of his true father. By the time you read this I will be dead, but I could not go to my grave taking with me a secret as powerful as this.

Below is my son's address. I therefore give you this information with my blessing, to do with what you will.

Yours

Joanna Wildman.

Beneath the woman's signature was the name 'Darian Wildman', and beneath that an address. A business address in London.

Shakily, Lara put the piece of paper back into the envelope. This was dramatic stuff. But then she had learned that drama and intrigue were part and parcel of anything to do with Maraban. Her best friend Rose had married Prince Khalim of Maraban, and through her Lara had caught glimpses of a life so very different from her own.

If someone else had opened such a letter what might they have done? Destroyed it and then forgotten about it? For didn't the existence of an unknown brother pose a threat to Khalim and his country? He might be older than Khalim and try to overthrow him.

Even thinking such thoughts they sounded far-fetched inside her own head, but they were not—they were true. For the mountain kingdom of Maraban inspired deep and dark passions which went hand in hand with its beauty and its turbulent history.

Slowly Lara rose to her feet, startled by her reflection in the beautiful looking-glass which hung over the huge fireplace. She looked so pale. Almost frightened. As if she had seen a ghost. But in a way maybe she had. Not *seen* a ghost, but learned about one.

Prince Khalim had a brother!

Oh, *why* hadn't someone else opened the letter? Then she would not have found herself in this awful dilemma of having information and not knowing what to do with it.

It would be so simple if the Prince wasn't married to Rose, but he was. Whether or not she liked it, she was involved, and that involvement had begun the moment her startled blue eyes had alighted on the stark words contained in the letter.

Lara stared out at the grey autumnal day, at the London traffic which moved slowly by, its sound muted by the thick bullet-proof windows, and thought once more about her friend.

Sometimes it still seemed incredible that Rose was now a princess and living in Maraban, with Khalim ruling at her side. Rose had been an ordinary girl, just like Lara herself—and yet look what had happened to her. Even now it still seemed like a fairy story that hadn't really happened.

Except that it *had* happened.

Just as this letter had been written and Lara had opened it.

It could be a lie. It could be a forgery. The author of the letter could be completely mad. A blackmailer. A potential assassin. Anything.

So what did she do?

Did she get on the phone to Rose and tell her that her husband could have an illegitimate brother?

But Rose was pregnant again. Think what the shock might do to her.

Should she go to the Ambassador? But surely that would

amount to the same thing—the first thing he would do would be to contact Khalim and tell him.

Still the thoughts continued to spin round and round in her head, unchecked until a solution occurred to her which was so blindingly simple she wondered why it had taken her so long to think of it.

What if *she*—Lara—went and found this Darian Wildman and sussed him out for herself? Almost as if she were sounding out the suitability of a would-be boyfriend.

Lara tucked the envelope into her handbag. If he was a good man then she would feel duty-bound to tell Rose and Khalim about him.

And if he wasn't?

Then she could destroy the letter and no one would be any the wiser.

Her heart pounded. Maybe she was being too simplistic, and playing God with information which had fallen into her hands quite by chance. And yet Khalim himself always said that nothing in life happened by chance, that everything happened for a reason. Only he called it something else. Lara racked her brain while she tried to remember what it was, and then she nodded.

Predestination. Yes, that was it. Predestination. Perhaps she had been *meant* to open the letter and to take the matter into her own hands.

Her mind drifted over the name. Darian Wildman. An intriguing name and an intriguing situation. She would find him. And see for herself just what kind of man he was.

But Lara's heart was beating very fast as she picked up the telephone and asked for Directory Enquiries.

Her thoughts were still reeling when she let herself into her apartment that evening to find Jake, her flatmate, cooking a fiery-looking concoction of curry.

He looked up and smiled as she walked into the sitting

room and threw her coat down on the sofa. 'I was about to ask if you'd had a hard day at the Embassy,' he joked. 'But judging from the look on your face I'd say it was a pretty redundant question. What's up, Lara? Has someone threatened to overthrow the Prince?'

'Shut up, Jake!' Lara bit her lip as the tight knot of tension somewhere in the pit of her stomach made itself known. 'Any chance of a drink?'

'Coming up—though I must say it's a little early for you, isn't it?' He slopped red wine into two glasses and handed her one, a slight frown creasing his brow. 'So what's up really?'

Lara sipped her wine thoughtfully, feeling the warmth flood through her, momentarily dissolving the sense of panic and trepidation she felt. Jake Haddon was the perfect flatmate—indeed, to almost every woman with a pulse he was the perfect man, full-stop. The darling of the British stage and screen, with his long legs and lazy charm and the lock of hair which flopped so endearingly over one of his soulful eyes and which had women itching to smooth it away for him. She had worked with him once but had never fancied him, which was fortunate given that he was now sharing her flat. He had moved in as a temporary measure, when he had been between homes and then had liked it so much that he'd never bothered moving out again. It felt like home, he told her.

And Lara didn't mind a bit. He was sweet and intelligent and trustworthy—even if he did sometimes tease her about Maraban and her friendship with its ruling family—yet, deep down, she knew she could not possibly confide in him about the letter, or her worries about the effect it might have on Khalim. He simply wouldn't take it seriously. In fact, sometimes she wondered if he ever took *anything* seriously.

But he was resourceful, she knew that—far more resourceful than she felt in this weird, jittering state of having discovered something momentous and not having a clue about what to do with that discovery.

'Jake?'

'Lara?'

'Just say…just say you wanted an introduction to someone and all you knew was the place where they worked—how would you go about meeting them?'

He batted his outrageously long lashes. 'This is a man, I take it?'

'Er, yes. How did you guess?'

'I know women,' said Jake smugly. 'And you have that kind of secretive, bursting excitement kind of look which immediately tells me that it's something to do with a member of the opposite sex. Am I right?'

That might be the easiest way to explain it, surely? Jake wouldn't ask too many questions if he thought she had a simple crush on a man.

'Sort of,' she prevaricated.

'Another actor?' he hazarded.

Lara shuddered. 'You know I'd sooner walk into a pit of deadly snakes than get involved with an actor!'

'Why, thanks,' he said wryly.

'You know what I mean, Jake.'

'Yeah, sure. Feckless commitment-phobes with fickle hearts—that's us actors!' He drank some wine and then gave the pot another stir. 'So who is he?'

Lara had been doing her homework. 'A businessman.'

'Successful?'

'I…think so.' The company was in Darian Wildman's name, which meant that he was successful, surely?

Jake's eyes narrowed. 'You haven't met him?'

'Er, no.'

'Curiouser and curiouser. What happened? You saw him at a party and were smitten, decided he was the man for you, but before you could do anything about it he'd left, yes? So you asked around a bit, found out his name, and now you're hot on his heels, pursuing him?'

'It was nothing like that,' Lara said weakly. 'And it's far too complicated to explain. I just want a chance to meet him, that's all.'

Jake threw a handful of coriander into the pot. 'Phone his office.'

'On what pretext?'

'Make something up! You're an enterprising woman, Lara—and you're an actress! Play it by ear—and once you're standing in front of him I am sure he will be completely dazzled by your wild dark hair and amazing blue eyes. The rest, as they say, is up to you!'

Lara finished her wine and held her glass out for a refill, studiously ignoring Jake's look of surprise—she rarely drank more than one, but tonight she felt she needed it. Could it be that simple? But why not? After all, what did she have to lose? She wasn't saying that you could know everything you needed to know about a person in one short meeting, but surely it would tell her whether he seemed a decent kind of man. And it would make up her mind whether she told him what she had discovered.

Or whether Khalim should hear about it first.

'That's very good thinking, Jake,' she said slowly. 'Very good thinking. I'll give it a go.'

'I don't know why you should sound so amazed!' he said drily. 'Just because I'm known for my boyish good looks doesn't mean that I don't have a few brain cells rattling around inside my head. Now, stop acting like I'm your servant and go and measure out some rice—that's if you want to eat this side of Christmas!'

She laughed and began to help him—he was so easy to get on with, but she knew deep down that was only because she didn't fancy him, nor he her. If she had, or he had, then their no-effort compatibility simply wouldn't exist. It wasn't that Lara was a cynic where men were concerned; she just preferred to think of herself as someone who was realistic.

They ate supper and watched a video of one of Jake's films, while he tore his own performance to pieces. In fact, Lara's resolve not to think any more about the situation lasted all the way until bedtime, but then she lay sleepless, looking at the ceiling for a long time, while moon shadows danced before her eyes and doubts began to creep into her mind.

She had the strangest feeling she was courting danger, as if she was standing on top of a high cliff and preparing to walk over the edge into the unknown—an unknown far more scary than just her usual uncertainty about the future. But that was just her imagination, she told herself as she finally drifted off to sleep. All actresses were cursed with an excess of imagination.

And in the morning everything looked different—as it so often did. It was funny how daylight seemed to put everything into perspective. She told herself that she was being stupid and ridiculously melodramatic—as if unable to separate her working life from her real life. Except that when she stopped to think about it 'real' life had taken on a very different meaning ever since her friend had married into Maraban's royal family!

Even Lara's mother had been taken aback by it all, and she was fairly used to the bizarre. In the past, if Lara had telephoned blithely to say that she was appearing as a tomato on a commerical for a new brand of soup, her mother had been merely interested. Yet for once she had been lost for words when Lara had announced that she was being Rose's bridesmaid when she married her prince, and would be wearing cloth of gold and a fortune in ancient jewellery for the day.

It had been easy enough to find the number of Wildman Phones, but not so easy to find the courage to dial the number, and when she did her nerve nearly failed her. But her drama training saved her. Pretend it's a job, she told herself—and maybe in a way it was. If not a job, then a mission—to be a good friend to people she cared about.

She drew a deep breath. The only way to get past receptionists was not to sound nervous or diffident but to brazen it out. 'Darian Wildman, please,' she said smoothly, as if she had known him all her life.

'I'm afraid that Mr Wildman is out of the office all day.'

Damn! Lara gave an exaggerated sigh. 'That man! Why the hell didn't he bother telling me? And he's left a whole stack of important papers behind,' she said, half to herself, then sighed and adopted a confidential one-woman-talking-to-another tone. 'Do you know where he can be reached?'

There was the briefest of pauses. 'Sure. He's out casting all day. Let me see...yep! Hold on, I've got the address here—do you have a pen?'

The receptionist obviously wouldn't have won any prizes for maintaining the privacy of her boss, thought Lara.

'Fire away,' she said calmly.

The receptionist rattled off an address in Golden Square, which Lara knew was right in the centre of London, just a breath away from Nelson's Column.

'What's he doing there?' Lara asked casually.

'Oh, he's been there all week—they're casting to find the face of Wildman Phones,' said the receptionist chattily. 'Why? Are you an actress or a model?'

Lara's heart gave a great leap in her chest, but she tried to keep the excitement from her voice. 'Well, actually,' she said, 'yes, I am.'

## CHAPTER TWO

THE taxi drew up outside a tall building which looked like an old warehouse—and that, thought Darian wryly, was precisely what it was. It was a dark, monstrous shell of a place which now housed the most modern of photographic studios.

'Shall we go in now, Darian?' asked the man by his side, his voice touched by a slight edge of anxiety.

Darian's eyes had been shuttered, but now they widened by a fraction so that just a glint of gold light gleamed from between the thick black lashes. He turned to look at Scott Stratton, the head of an advertising agency known to be one of the best in the business—famous for its slick, award-winning campaigns and its ability to match client needs with consumer expectations. Or at least it had been up until now, when casting after casting had so far stubbornly refused to find the new face of Wildman Phones. Maybe Darian was being too choosy—an accusation which had been thrown at him often enough in the past—but he was certainly uncompromising, and he would not be satisfied until he found exactly what he was looking for. He just wasn't sure quite what that was.

Or who.

'Sure, Scott,' he murmured. 'I'm ready.'

Scott glanced at him. 'Need anything? To make notes?'

Darian gave a glittering smile. 'No, thanks. I won't need them. I'll know her when I see her.'

They walked into the building together, and stood in the chrome-walled reception area.

'They're all up there?' asked Darian, jerking his dark head towards the spiral staircase which led up to the studio.

He spoke softly, but even so the two women who were busy flicking through the models' cards at the far end of the room immediately stopped what they were doing and turned round to look at him, as if awaiting a command. But then, people always did that when they encountered him. Darian was used to it. They seemed to shrink to his will whenever he exerted it—and even when he didn't.

'Yeah,' answered Scott. 'Ready and waiting.'

'Then bring on the parade,' said Darian mockingly, putting his foot on the bottom rung of the staircase, faded denim straining over one taut, muscular thigh as he did so.

'Er, not *parade*, Darian,' corrected Scott. 'If you say that they *parade* then that makes them sound a bit mindless, doesn't it? Makes them sound as if they're taking part in some second-rate beauty contest, and models are very sensitive about that kind of thing. Particularly in these politically correct days.'

Darian laughed and turned his head, and as he did so he heard the faint but unmistakable intake of breath from one of the secretaries as she looked at him. He was used to that, too. He guessed it was because his eyes were not run-of-the-mill that the fairer sex always seemed to get transfixed by them. When he was younger he had found the effect a little disconcerting, and later he had rather enjoyed it, but now he was so used to it as to feel nothing more than faint amusement. Another man might have used the power of those eyes more ruthlessly, but Darian did not. He had no need to.

'Far be it from me to contradict you, Scott,' he said, choosing his words carefully. 'But, putting political correctness aside, surely a casting session is exactly like a beauty contest? Though admittedly not a second-rate one—not in this case—not if they're going to be representing Wildman. Twenty females about to be assessed on their looks and their sex appeal—how else would you define it?'

'But it isn't just looks and sex appeal we're searching for, is it?' questioned Scott seriously. 'Otherwise someone we've shown you already would surely have come up to standard?' He sighed. 'You've seen loads of beautiful women this week.'

'You think I'm being too choosy?' asked Darian.

Scott shrugged and then shook his head. 'I admire your perfectionism, if you must know. Your search for that indefinable something or someone—a person who will embody everything you want to say about your company. I guess that's the secret of your success. Am I right?'

Darian shrugged. 'That's part of it.'

But only part. Darian put a lot of his success down to a restless and relentless seeking nature. He never did anything long enough to get bored, because when you were bored all the freshness and enjoyment simply vanished. It was the same with relationships. Familiarity, in his experience, bred a tedium far more deadly than contempt.

He glanced at his watch. 'Come on, then—let's go.'

They made their way up the winding staircase towards the studio.

None of the people who worked for him knew yet that this advertising campaign was to be Darian's swansong. First he would choose the perfect woman and with her face bombard the country with the name of his mobile phones to ensure maximum publicity.

Then he wanted out. He was planning to sell the company and walk away. To take the money and add it to the pile he had already made by selling previous successful companies, and look for yet another new challenge.

And then what? prompted a little voice in his head. Is that going to bring you happiness? Darian's mouth curved into a sardonic smile, and he batted the thought away as if it had been a mildly troublesome fly. Men who sought happiness were doomed. Women, too. Success and achievement were far more tangible concepts than happiness as far as Darian was concerned.

They were almost at the top of the flight of steps when he heard Scott's slightly muffled voice from behind him. 'We should announce you, really, Darian—shouldn't we?'

'Well, you could, I suppose,' said Darian lazily, but then he shook his head. 'No, on second thoughts—don't. Let's surprise them.'

'Sure?'

Unseen, Darian smiled. 'Oh, perfectly sure,' he said softly. 'Women are always so much more *interesting* when you catch them unawares, don't you think? You see them for what they really are, rather than what they want you to see.'

'That sounds like a pretty harsh judgement,' observed Scott. 'I didn't have you down for a cynic.'

Darian smiled again, but this time it barely curved his lips. 'Not harsh at all,' he said softly. 'Nor cynical. Just an accurate assessment. Now, come on—let's go.' And as his dark head appeared in the lighted studio the whole room fell silent.

Lara was out of breath, her unruly hair looking even more tousled than usual. The denim jacket she wore was making her much too hot, but she didn't want to spare the time to take it off. She waited for the bus to swish its way through the puddle past her, and then made a run for the door of the studio, glancing at her watch as she did so. Damn, damn and damn!

Her agent had been doubtful—sniffy, even—about putting Lara forward for the casting, but frantic questioning had assured her that, yes, there was a last vacant slot in the day's casting for Wildman Phones.

'Why the hell didn't you put me forward for it in the first place?' she had wailed.

Her agent had sounded incredulous. 'Lara—the last time I saw you your hair was cropped and dark.'

'But I was appearing in a Russian play!' she'd protested. 'It's back to normal now!'

'How normal is normal?' her agent had enquired patiently. 'You're a brunette, lovie—and they're looking for the archetypal English rose!'

'Archetypal, not stereotypical!' Lara had retorted. 'There's nothing in the rulebook to say an English rose can't have dark hair!'

'I suppose *not,*' her agent had responded doubtfully.

Lara pushed the studio door open and a brief feeling of irony washed over her. English rose indeed! Clad in denim and a clinging black tee-shirt, anyone less fitting the description she had yet to see. But she reminded herself that she wasn't really here to get the job. She was here to see the great man himself, that was all—and what better way to do that than legitimately?

The two women standing in the foyer looked her up and down.

'Which way's the casting?' Lara squeaked.

One looked uncertain and the other gave a slightly smug smile as she jerked her thumb in the direction of the spiral staircase. 'Up there. And you're late,' she added bluntly.

'I know I am,' moaned Lara, as she legged it up the steps.

The room was stifling, reeked of lots of different clashing perfumes, and was full of women. Correction—beautiful women. And every single one of them had taken to heart the English rose theme in a big, big way. Despite her nerves, Lara bit back a smile.

Some of them wore lace-trimmed blouses; others were resplendent in flower-sprigged high-necked dresses. There was even one woman clad in floor-length muslin who looked as if she would be more at home eating cucumber sandwiches on a quintessential English lawn, instead of packed into a crowded studio with a load of competitive peers.

And every woman in the room shared one unmistakable characteristic.

They were all blonde!

'S-sorry!' gulped Lara as each sleek golden head turned in her direction.

Then, just as quickly, the women turned away from her again, and it took a moment or two while she caught her breath for Lara to realise that they were now all looking at one person. Or, rather, one man.

Lara hadn't noticed him at first, because he had been standing in the shadows in one corner of the room, but once she had seen him she wondered how on earth he could have escaped her attention—because he seemed to radiate a vitality which made everyone else in the room look as though they were only half-alive. She narrowed her eyes in his direction and felt her heart clench in her chest, as if an iron fist had crumpled it between cold, hard fingers.

'I—I'm l-late,' she stammered.

'Damn right you are,' he agreed, in a silky murmur.

She kept her face composed—she never quite knew how she did it—not when she was feeling this faint and dizzy and weak—and surreptitiously snaked her tongue out over lips which had dried so thoroughly that she felt she would never be able to speak again.

Sometimes you knew the truth about something by instinct alone, and if she had ever doubted the claim made by the writer of that letter then that doubt was vanquished instantly as she stared across the room at Darian Wildman.

Was it just her imagination working overtime—fuelled by the information she had received—or was everyone else in the room, Darian included, blind to what was as obvious as the blazing glare from one of the studio lights?

This man had royal blood running through his veins, setting him apart from everyone present. Marking him out as a different breed altogether—as different as a lion standing amid a group of mewing kittens.

He was tall—impressively tall—even taller than Khalim—yet his skin was not so dark as Khalim's. But then this man was only half-Marabanese, Lara remembered. His flesh glowed gold and tawny and his eyes were gold, too. She had never seen eyes like them—they were like shards of golden glass, deep and gleaming, except that gold was a warm colour and this man's eyes were cold.

His hair was very dark—though not quite black—and was shaped to a head which was held with confidence and a certain arrogance. And pride. And irritation.

'Do you make a habit of turning up late for jobs?' he questioned tersely.

Lara was having to fight an uncomfortable desire to run over to him, whisper her fingertips wonderingly down the side of his hard, beautiful face and tell him that she alone had the secret of his ancestry.

With an effort, she pulled herself together. 'Of course not!'

Her complete absence of an apology made Darian tense, and he narrowed his eyes, feeling the tiny hairs prickle at the back of his neck as he looked at her. Her rain-sprinkled dark hair was awry and her cheeks were flushed. And her eyes were the bluest he had ever seen. They made him think of summer skies and cornflowers and Mediterranean seas. Momentarily, and inexplicably, he was sucked in by the sheer beauty of those eyes and the distraction irritated him.

'And are you in the habit of poor time-keeping?'

Be bold, Lara, she thought. You don't need this job.

She shrugged. 'Not usually.'

Not *usually*? It was not the reaction that Darian had been expecting. Didn't she care that there were women in this room who looked as if they would kill to get the job? And, judging from some of the shameless glances they had been directing at him, they would also offer far more sensual incentives if they thought that might work.

'Looking as if you've been dragged through a hedge backwards?' he continued, in an acid tone.

'So much for the tousled look!' retorted Lara flippantly. 'Actually, the reason I'm late is that my agency nearly didn't send me.'

He met the challenge in her gaze, and something about her directness made him carry on staring at her. He wasn't used to a challenge—and certainly not from a woman.

'I'm not surprised,' he said softly.

She arched her brows, hot and bothered and not just from her hurried journey. Something in the way those gold eyes were studying her made her wish that she was looking as cool and unflappable as every other woman in the room. But Lara knew that nobody could guess what you were feeling on the inside; it was what you projected from the outside that counted. Which meant that her one-word reply shot back at him sounded cool, and only just on the right side of insolent. 'Really?'

'Yes, really,' he mocked. 'The brief was to look like an English rose,' he added impatiently. 'Since when did that entail looking as if you're in the middle of hitching a ride to a rock concert?'

Lara heard a little buzz from the other models, and she

guessed that they were enjoying seeing the delectable Mr Wildman losing his cool with one of the competition. She glared at him.

'Do you want me to ask her to leave, Darian?' murmured Scott, in a low voice.

'No, I don't,' demurred Darian. 'I asked a question and I'm waiting for an answer.'

She felt like asking him sweetly if he always got whatever it was he wanted, but she refrained. It was neither the time nor the place, and she suspected that the answer would be yes anyway.

'It depends what your interpretation of an English rose *is,* surely?' she answered confidently. 'Even *they* have to run for taxis or buses sometimes, don't they? They can't spend the whole of their lives sitting on pretty wicker furniture and fanning themselves! Not modern English roses anyway!'

There it was again, he thought, with a cross between grudging admiration and irritation. She was talking to him in a way which he could have confidently predicted no one else in the room would have *dared* try! And she did have a point, he conceded. Modern was what he was really looking for. A modern look for modern technology.

Ask for someone who summed up everything that it was to be English, and everyone immediately jumped back a century or two! He glanced around the room at the lace and the flower-sprigs and the muslin and he frowned. Modern and English—surely the two weren't completely incompatible?

'You do have a point,' he admitted grudgingly.

Lara lifted her chin, telling herself that she definitely wasn't going to get the job now, so what did she have to lose? How far could she push him? She had seen for herself that he was grumpy—as well as successful, powerful and devastatingly attractive—would his temper really turn ugly if she challenged him a little bit more?

'Tell me, how do *you* see the woman you're looking for?' asked Lara calmly.

Scott bristled. 'I think you've said quite enough, don't you?'

But Darian shook his head. 'No, let her speak.'

'Gosh...*thanks*!' said Lara sarcastically.

Darian knitted his brows together, wondering if this rather unusual tendency to answer back at what was essentially a serious job interview was simply a way of getting herself noticed. Didn't people sometimes act outrageously in order to detract attention from their glaring faults? And did she have any?

He let his eyes travel from the top of her head to the tips of her pointed leather boots. If you discounted the fact that her hair looked as though she had spent a large part of the morning being pulled through a particularly thorny hedge it really was the most glorious colour—the deep, burnished mahogany of a lovingly polished piece of furniture, touched with deeper, brighter shades of gold and amber. Dyed, most probably. All women dyed their hair these days. His mouth twisted. He had yet to meet a *natural* blonde!

But her brows were beautifully shaped and arched, and her skin looked soft—all roses and cream—like petals in the early morning when they had been kissed by the dew. It was skin that made her look as though she'd been brought up in the fresh air, raised on nothing stronger than milk and honey.

She had answered her own question, he realised. She was exactly the woman he was looking for.

'Take your jacket off,' he said slowly.

For a second Lara's sang-froid almost deserted her. It was a perfectly normal request to make in the circumstances. It wasn't as though he was asking her to perform a striptease. But that was exactly what it felt like. Inside, she was suddenly overcome with a bubbling mass of insecurity, which was crazy—*crazy*—and yet there was something about this darkly golden man which made his request seem like an intrusion. She didn't move.

Darian raised his eyebrows questioningly, ignoring Scott's frown and the indignant glances of the other women.

Lara flashed him a cool and professional smile and slid her jacket from her shoulders with hands which were miraculously steady. Then casually slipped her finger through the loop of the jacket and stood before him, feeling a little as she imagined the favoured member of a harem must feel. All the women vying for one man's attention and only one of them receiving it. Her heart was beating fast. You're concocting fantasy, she told herself sternly. That's all. Just because you think he's the brother of the Sheikh you're attributing to him all those kind of primitive man-woman things which you wouldn't dream of doing if he was any average man.

'How's that?' she asked, in a voice which she hoped didn't betray quite how unsettled he was making her feel.

'That's fine,' he said evenly, trying to be objective, but for once it wasn't easy. Her body was good. Very good. She was tall and slender, and yet curved in just the right places, and her breasts were quite simply perfect—not too full and not too small, the white tee-shirt emphasising their shape and not quite disguising the pinpoint thrust of her nipples, which made him tense in desire even though he tried not to.

Darian looked around at the others. In terms of beauty there was not one woman present who could be faulted. There was every variety of womanhood represented here today. Most were slim—too slim, in his opinion, but that was the fashion. True, there were a couple whose curves were more luscious than slim, but the camera didn't flatter real curves; he knew that.

Leisurely, he ran his eyes over each and every one of them, until they came back to rest and stay on the girl in the jeans. She looked normal and healthy and glowing and…and something about her was still making his skin tingle.

He nodded and turned to Scott. 'Can I have a word, please? In private?' he asked him.

'Sure,' Scott replied.

The two men moved to the only vacant corner of the studio. 'I think we've found our English rose,' Darian said slowly. 'Don't you?'

Scott turned to him. 'But she's a *brunette*!'

'So? I don't remember specifically asking for blonde!'

Scott lowered his voice. 'We haven't even tested her yet, Darian,' he said, a touch anxiously. 'In fact, we haven't tested any of them.'

Darian gave an arrogant shrug. 'There's no need. She's the one I want.'

'But she might project completely the wrong image.'

Darian studied the varying blondes in the studio, who were all looking at him hopefully. They looked…they looked…*bland*, he realised impatiently. He flicked another glance at the brunette, who seemed so full of life and vitality in comparison, and a steady pulse began to beat at his temple. 'She won't,' he said steadily. 'Trust me.'

'The place will erupt if you don't test the others, too,' protested Scott.

Darian shrugged. 'Then test them.'

'And show you the results?'

'If you want. I'll see them, but I won't need to.'

'How can you be so sure?'

Darian gave a slow smile. Instinct. Simple as that. She had what he wanted. 'I just am. She's the one.'

The atmosphere in the room was electric, and Lara felt decidedly odd. This wasn't like a normal casting at all. Everyone was staring at her, and she wondered if the composition of her body had undergone some remarkable transformation, whether her blood could suddenly have become jelly. Because that was what she felt like—that was the way *he* was making her feel.

The man with the golden eyes had turned back and was staring at her, and Lara felt as though she was helpless, caught in the honeyed intensity of that gaze. Like a rabbit hypnotised and blinded by the glaring headlights of a car, or a snake lured and seduced by the sound of the charmer's pipe.

'What's your name?' he asked softly.

Lara took a deep breath. She just knew that he was going to offer her the job! This couldn't really be happening. It shouldn't be happening. She had turned up late, looking scruffy, and been rude to him—he should be sending her packing, not seriously entertaining the thought of employing her! But she kept her voice steady—as steady as his golden stare. 'Lara. Lara Black.'

'Lara Black,' he repeated thoughtfully. 'Yes.' He gave the room a cool smile. 'Well, I'll leave you all in the capable hands of Scott.'

He moved away, and Lara watched him as he placed one foot on the staircase. He glanced up at that moment and their eyes met, and she was suddenly filled with an inexplicable feeling of disappointment and stupidity.

Was that it, then? She bit her lip distractedly. What had she expected? That he would suddenly announce to everyone that she had got the job without bothering to test the others? As if that would happen! Especially to someone who had behaved with such utter disregard for professionalism.

She felt a stupid sense of loss as she watched his dark, lustrous head disappear from view. He had gone and she had blown any chance of getting to know him better. But she knew one thing for sure.

He was Khalim's brother. The resemblance was unmistakable.

So what was she going to do about it?

# CHAPTER THREE

LARA put the phone down and stared at Jake. 'I've got it,' she said slowly.

Jake looked up from the script he was studying. 'Got what?'

'That job I went for. You know—I told you.'

Jake frowned. 'Something about a mobile phone company? You turned up late, looking ghastly, and the owner was there and subjected you to a grilling?'

It was still taking a moment or two to sink in. 'That's right.'

Jake elevated one brow in a manner which would have caused almost any other woman in the country to swoon, but not Lara.

'Does this guy have a death wish?' he joked. 'Or does he just like a challenge?'

Lara didn't say anything. She suspected that Darian Wildman *did* like a challenge, and something about that worried her—though it now appeared that her gut reaction had been the correct one, after all. She had *thought* that he was going to offer her the job, but then he had just disappeared and left them all to be photographed. Still, when she mulled it over now, he couldn't possibly have done otherwise, could he? Not employed her without testing her and, more importantly, without testing all the others—otherwise he would have had a small riot on his hands.

Yet she had sensed that he was about to do so. He looked like the kind of man who broke all the rules and made his own up. The word autocratic might have been invented with him in mind. It had probably been the other man with him, she reasoned, who had persuaded him to adopt the usual method of casting.

She should have been overjoyed. This was *work*, after all, and she needed to work—especially as the person she'd been covering for at the Embassy was now much better and ready to go back to her job. And she was supposed to be finding out more about Darian Wildman—so wasn't this a heaven-sent opportunity to do just that? To work for his company and to become the face which symbolised that company.

Except it didn't feel like that. It felt uncomfortable. Wrong. As if she was doing something that she shouldn't be doing. And coupled with that was the burden of the knowledge she possessed.

Or maybe it had something to do with the fact that Darian had excited her in a way that no man had excited her for longer than she could remember. And that in itself was a *bad sign*. One which made her feel gloomy about him in general. If she was attracted to him then he was *bound* to be trouble, because Lara's track record with men was nothing short of abysmal.

She didn't fall for men very often, but when she did it was always for the kind of man your mother warned you to stay away from. Philanderers and cheats. Good-looking, weak, shallow men. The sort who promised you the earth and a little bit more besides, and then were busy glancing over your shoulder to see if someone more attractive had just walked in. In fact, she had sworn off men altogether—at least until she had worked out what was the basic flaw in her character which attracted her to the wrong type of man.

Her friend Rose had a few theories of her own. She said that it was because Lara yearned for excitement and was looking for it in the wrong places—but how on earth could you go looking for it in the *right* places if solid and decent men—the kind your mother *would* approve of—left you cold?

'Oh, you need a sheikh, like Khalim,' Rose had laughed on the eve of her wedding.

At the time Lara had been struggling into a dress which weighed almost as much as she did. 'Don't be so smug!'

'But I'm not,' Rose had protested, and had laid her hand on Lara's shoulder, her voice gentling. 'I'm serious. It's just a pity that Khalim hasn't got any brothers.'

Lara chewed on her lip. Oh, Lord—she had completely forgotten that conversation until now! But that was the cleverness of the mind, wasn't it?—It dragged things up from the hidden corners of your subconscious when it thought they might come in useful. If only Rose had known how eerily prescient her words had been.

If it had been anyone other than Khalim then it might have been easy to pick up the phone and say, Hi, guess what? I've discovered you have a secret half-brother! But Khalim was no normal man. He was Sheikh of a vast kingdom, and if another man was related to him by blood, then couldn't he lay claim to that kingdom and jeopardise the livelihood of all of them? His and Rose's and their son's, and the child soon to be born? How could she knowingly endanger all that until she knew something of the man himself?

'Lara?'

She looked up to see Jake staring at her with concern. 'What?'

'You've gone as white as a sheet.'

'Have I?' She touched her cheek and found that it was cold, and suddenly she began to shiver. 'We shoot on Monday,' she whispered.

On Monday she would see him again. Those strangely cold golden eyes would pierce right through her and see…

Would they sense that she was not all she seemed? And how would he react if she told him that *he* was not all he seemed, either?

Jake frowned. 'Lara, what *is* the matter? You've just won a fantastic contract—why aren't you cracking open the champagne?'

She forced a smile. Why not, indeed? Perhaps she was simply guilty of inventing problems where there were none. 'Coming right up,' she said brightly, and headed for the fridge.

The winter sun streamed in through the glass, warming his skin as Darian slowly buttoned up his white linen shirt and watched an aeroplane creeping across the sky in the far distance. Outside, the clouds were tinged with pink and gold, contrasting with an ice-blue sky which made the world look as perfect as it was supposed to look. But then the views from his penthouse apartment were always matchless and magnificent and never the same. It was one of the reasons he had bought it—that and its inaccessibility to people in general and the world in particular.

The phone rang, but he let it ring. Most phone calls, in his experience, could be usefully avoided, and he hated having to make small-talk—especially in the mornings. Which was one of the reasons why it was a long time since he had stayed overnight with a woman.

He listened to the message on the answer-machine, to hear the voice of the travel agent telling him that his flight to New York was confirmed, and smiled. If he *had* picked it up then he would have had to endure all kinds of bright and unnecessary questions about the state of his health!

He picked up his coffee cup and sipped thoughtfully at the strong, inky brew, glancing over at the mirror as he did so. There was no sign of blood. Not now. He gave a tiny grimace. What was going on? He had cut himself shaving that morning—lightly nicked the skin around his jaw—something he could not remember doing since he was an adolescent boy, when he had first wielded the razor with uncertain fingers.

In his gleaming bathroom mirror he had stared at the bright spot of scarlet which had beaded on the strong line of his jaw, disrupting his normal, ordered routine, and it had taken him right back to a place he rarely visited.

The past. That strange place over which you had little control and yet whose influence shaped the person you would be for the rest of your life.

He had never been one of those boys who had shaved before there was any need to. It was simply that he had seemed to develop way ahead of anyone else, with a faint shadowing of the jaw when most of his peers were still covered in spots. He had shot up in height, too, and his shoulders had grown broad and his body hard and muscular.

Such early maturity had set him apart—especially with the girls—but then, in a way he had felt set apart ever since he could remember. He had never looked like anyone else, even though his clothes had been no different. His skin had always had a faintly tawny glow to it, and his golden eyes had marked him out as someone different.

The girls had loved it and the boys had tried teasing him because of it, but he had quickly learnt that his height and strength could intimidate them enough to stop the insults almost before they had started.

So his childhood had been lonely. The only child of a single mother, bringing him up in a seedy apartment in one of the wastelands of London where tourists never ventured. That in itself had not been unusual—poverty had brought with it all the casualties of human relationships, and Darian had known only a couple of sets of parents who had still been together—and they had fought enough to make him wonder why they bothered.

He guessed it was that at least other kids had *known* who their father was. Whether it was the father who had run off with a younger woman, or the father who would appear threateningly drunk on his former family's doorstep, or the father who refused to pay money the courts had told him he must pay. These were fathers it was easy enough to hate, but Darian's own paternity had been one big secret. He would rather have had someone to hate than no one at all.

He had tried asking his mother about it, but even broaching the subject had made her mouth tremble, as if she was about to cry—and she never cried. He had learnt only that some questions were better left unasked…

The doorbell jangled, disrupting his thoughts. His driver was here. Darian picked up his jacket, feeling an almost imperceptible glow of subdued excitement as he sat back in the soft leather luxury of the car. He told himself it was because they were shooting the photos today, and that something which no longer challenged him was coming to an end, but he knew that was not the whole story.

The truth was that he wanted to see the model again. What was her name? Lara. Yes, that was it. Pretty name and a pretty girl. Fearless and spiky. He rubbed his eyes and closed them as the car began to accelerate, stretching his long legs out in front of him and yawning lazily.

He was tired. He had sat up until the early hours, sorting through his accounts and feeling bored—with pretty much everything. Appetites which were fed with everything they needed tended to become jaded, he told himself ruefully.

He wondered when his life had become like a game of Monopoly—just a load of numbers that were so big they didn't seem real. But that was the way of money—too much and it almost seemed to get in the way, not enough and it dominated your whole life and all your thoughts. Was there no simple in-between way?

He guessed there was—the way most men chose. Marriage and babies and a house in the suburbs. Daily train journeys and home for supper and a drink. Weekend barbecues and driving out to pretty country pubs.

But to Darian it sounded like a lifetime's incarceration. A cell padded with sofas and chintz curtains. Maybe that was why he had never even come close to commitment, because commitment carried with it the price of settling down and raising a family. That was the way of things. In fact, no one had ever stirred his blood enough to make him even *think* of committing, or to make him feel a pang of regret that he was unable to.

*You will be a lonely old man,* taunted a little voice inside his head, but even that didn't bother him. Lonely and alone were two entirely different concepts, weren't they? He felt as if he had been alone for all his life, so why change now? Even if change was possible, and Darian didn't think it was. That was the mistake that people always made—women especially. They thought that a person could change the habits of a lifetime and become the someone they wanted you to be.

The driver turned his head as Big Ben loomed up magnificently in front of them. 'Do you want me to wait?'

Darian shook his head. 'No, thanks. I'll ring when I need you. I may hang around for a while,' he added casually.

He told himself that he liked to be in control—which was true—and that he liked to be hands-on—which was also true. If there was going to be an advertising campaign then he wanted to have some input into the final images which would represent his company.

But most of all he wanted to watch Lara at work, to see

her thick dark hair blowing in the autumn breeze and see the sky reflected in eyes which echoed its hue.

Lara Black.

The English rose.

Lara noticed him before he saw her. The heavens themselves seemed to be conniving in his entrance, because just as his long legs began to emerge from a seriously luxurious car a shaft of pure golden sunlight chose that very moment to spear its way through the fluffy clouds. And he chose just that same instant to look up, his eyes vying with the sun for brilliance.

Lara shivered.

'Keep still, Lara,' said the make-up artist patiently as she dabbed on another stroke of pink iridescent lipgloss.

Lara couldn't reply, not with her lips half open to deal with the lipgloss, but she was aware of him approaching, silent and stealthy—like a natural predator. The sharp colours of the autumn day seemed to emphasise his strong features—etching shadows which fell from beneath the high cheekbones and the firm, luscious mouth.

He wore linen, which managed to be both casual and smart at the same time. Yet somehow it looked all wrong on him, and she wondered what he would look like with the fluid, silken robes of the Maraban aristocracy clinging to his lean, hard frame.

She could hear the chatter lessening as the make-up artist turned her head to see what what was happening and whistled softly. She gave Lara's lips a final blot with a piece of tissue.

'Oh, *wow,*' she whispered fervently. 'I wouldn't mind getting my hands on *him!*'

Lara gave her chin a welcome stretch, but her heart thudded painfully in her chest. 'You mean from a professional point of view, of course?' she joked.

'Yeah, sure.' The make-up artist gave a rich and fruity

laugh. 'One look at him and all I think about is work, work, work!'

Lara watched him while the stylist fussed around with her dress. Little clusters of people had stopped to stare at the proceedings, alerted to the possibility of excitement by the photographer and his acolytes and the sight of a woman wearing a floaty, filmy dress on a blustery autumn day.

'Are you making a film?' she heard one middle-aged shopper ask.

'A photo-shoot,' drawled the photographer's assistant, with a shake of his long hair.

But Lara felt as though they might have been aliens from another planet—she felt disconnected and oblivious to just about everything except for him, which was more than a little bit scary. She tried to tell herself that *of course* she was going to be interested in him—that was the whole point of her presence here. But surely that wouldn't account for the pounding of her heart and the silken throb of her blood which seemed to strike soft hammerblows at all her pulse-points. Not by anyone's standards could *that* be described as professional behaviour.

Maybe the make-up artist had put it in a nutshell. Think Darian Wildman and the last thing you felt was professional.

She turned away, breaking the spell with an effort. The last thing she needed was for him to look up and see her staring at him like some kind of starstruck adolescent. There were enough people already doing that.

'We're never going to keep your hair under control with this breeze!' grumbled the stylist as she pushed a wayward strand off Lara's face.

'Looks perfect to me,' came a slow, deep voice from behind her.

Lara tried to count to ten, but the numbers became jumbled in her mind as she turned round. At least the half-smile on her lips was appropriate, as was the polite, almost deferential raising of her eyebrows. After all, he was the boss and she the model.

'Hi,' she said.

'Hi.' He found himself mocking her, enjoying the brief moment of discomfiture which allowed itself to break through her cool little smile, but then his eyes narrowed. Maybe she was used to men coming onto her. With looks like that she was bound to be. He saw her shiver. 'You're cold,' he said softly.

Lara looked down at the goose bumps on her arms, which was infinitely easier than meeting that clear golden stare, and composed herself enough to look up again, a rueful smile playing on her lips. 'Well, yes,' she agreed. 'Silk chiffon is a wonderful floaty fabric, but it wasn't exactly designed with warmth in mind!'

'No.' He forced himself to be objective. He had sat in with the creative team while they thrashed around the kind of image they wanted to project. Delicate and ethereal had been the objective—an objective achieved perfectly on the mock-ups they had shown him.

But reality, in the flesh and blood form of Lara Black, had an impact he had not been expecting. A bone-melting, sensual impact. Maybe that had been the subtle difference which had marked her out from all the others, Darian thought—that understated but persuasive femininity which could overpower men by stealth.

'Do you want a jacket or something?' he asked suddenly.

The question took Lara off-guard, and for one mad moment she thought he was actually going to take off his own jacket and offer it to her! As if! Lara pointed to a soft pink wrap which lay draped over one of the canvas chairs. 'I have a shawl. I'll—'

'Here—let me.' He bent and scooped the garment up, and draped it around her shoulders, feeling her shiver as he did so. 'You really *are* cold,' he observed, feeling the smoothness of her skin through the fine cashmere.

'Yes.' But that was not the reason she had shivered. She knew that, and she suspected he knew that, too. It seemed like the most deliciously old-fashioned and chivalrous act—a disarming act—to put her shawl on for her like that. A man like Darian Wildman would be aware of that. Talk to him, she told herself. This is your opportunity!

'Do you…do you often go on shoots like this?' she ventured.

The lips curved into a cool smile. 'Is that a take on the "do you come here often" line?' he mocked.

At that moment Lara hated him for making her feel so unoriginal, but she didn't show it, shrugging her shoulders instead. 'Don't answer if you don't want to,' she murmured. 'I'd hate to think I was straying into unprotected waters!'

He laughed. This was better. He liked her spiky better than he liked her soft. Softness made women vulnerable, and vulnerable women weren't equals. They got hurt, and then they made you feel bad because of it. 'Was I being rude?' he mused.

'Yes.'

He raised his eyebrows fractionally, taken aback by her blunt reply. 'The answer to your question is no—but then I rarely conduct advertising campaigns.'

'So why this one?'

He wasn't about to start telling *her* about his plan to float Wildman on the stockmarket—she, like the rest of the world, would find out about it soon enough. 'Because I want the name Wildman to be synonymous with mobile phone technology.'

'You mean it isn't already?' she teased. 'Shame on you!'

He allowed his mouth to curve into a small smile. 'I know. Shocking, isn't it?' he questioned gravely.

'Utterly,' she agreed, realising that he was flirting with her and that she was flirting right back.

Their eyes met and he regarded her thoughtfully. He wanted to take her out to dinner, he realised, not exchange snatches of conversation while the crew ran around, shouting and disrupting them. And just then, as if echoing his thoughts, someone shouted her name.

He frowned. 'Sounds like you're needed,' he observed.

'Sounds that way.' She hugged the shawl tightly around her as the stylist beckoned, hoping that she didn't sound reluctant to leave. 'Excuse me,' she murmured, glad to get away because nothing seemed to be going according to plan—although when she stopped to think about it what plan had she actually made, other than to somehow get to meet him? And now that she had managed to do that, all she could do was fantasise about his golden eyes and his lean, hard body. It just wasn't good enough.

Darian watched while the stylist fussed around with Lara's hair and then the photographer moved over, whipped the wrap away and began to coax her into position, prowling around in front of her, crooning directions.

'That's right, baby—smile! Not too much—just a kind of cool, thoughtful smile, as if you're deciding whether to dump your lover or not!'

Lara smiled.

'That's good! Now half close your eyes—as if you're trying to drive him wild with jealousy! You're thinking of another man—and you want him more!'

Lara did as she was told, her eyelashes fluttering down, finding it remarkably easy, picturing golden eyes and tawny skin and a dark, burnished head of royal descent...

She snapped her eyes open, startled as the bright flash exploded, staring into the eyes of the man who was fantasy and yet real, and for a moment the rest of the world receded.

Darian stared back at her, and for the first time in his life he recognised the intrusiveness of the camera and despised the intimacy it created between photographer and subject. For a moment there she had looked so sexually excited that it might almost have been for real. His mouth tightened. What a way to earn a living, he thought in sudden disgust. Yet it was what he wanted, wasn't it?

No. It was what his *company* wanted. And this was an assignment, he reminded himself. A professional assignment. He hadn't been introduced to her at a party—maybe if he had it might be different. Instead, he had run across her in the course of work, and he kept the line between work and pleasure strictly delineated.

Lara saw his face harden and wondered what had happened to the courteous man who had wrapped the soft wool around her shoulders. The golden eyes had darkened, a flush of colour was running along the high, aristocratic cheekbones. For a moment she saw the glimmerings of a hard, almost cruel contempt, and his expression filled her with trepidation even while something feminine ached at the very core of her, revelling in that cold look of mastery.

With an effort she tore her gaze away from him, staring instead at the phtographer, giving the shot everything she had and suddenly wishing that she was a million miles away from that hard, glittering scrutiny.

She held her arms aloft and the silk chiffon twirled and clung to her thighs. Abruptly, he turned away, and she forced herself to concentrate on the job in hand, losing herself in it because that seemed infinitely easier than losing herself in the gaze of Darian Wildman.

But when the photographer had stopped shooting there was no sign of him.

'Where's Darian?' she questioned casually as she pulled the wrap back round her shoulders.

'Gone,' said the assistant.

She hadn't even noticed him leaving, and she was surprised by a great, swamping feeling of disappointment. Gone! There were five other London locations to get through and suddenly the day seemed to stretch away endlessly in front of her.

Had she thought that he would be accompanying them to Tower Bridge and the Mall and Leadenhall Market and the other places which had been carefully chosen each to reflect a different mood of London life?

But perhaps this was best—he was a distracting man in anyone's book.

Lara channelled all her frustration into getting exactly the poses which the photographer demanded, and tried not to think about whether she would see him again, and where she went from here if she did not.

It was dark by the time she arrived back at the apartment and Jake was at home, all dandied up in a stunning black dinner jacket, swearing softly as he attempted to subdue his bow-tie.

'Do this for me, would you, Lara?'

She put her bag down, knotted the black silk into a neat bow, and stood back. 'How's that?'

'Perfect.' He made another small, unnecessary adjustment. 'Someone rang for you,' he said casually as she flopped onto the sofa with a heavy sigh.

'Oh?'

'A man.'

'Oh, again,' said Lara uninterestedly. But something about the amused curiosity in his voice made her sit up. 'Did he leave a message?'

'He did.'

'Jake—stop playing games! Who was it and what did he say?'

Jake enunciated his words carefully. 'His name is Darian Wildman and he says he'll call you tomorrow.'

## CHAPTER FOUR

WHY was it, Lara wondered, that whenever you wanted someone to telephone you, they didn't—and the opposite was always true?

And why had he rung at all? Had he already seen the finished photos and decided he didn't like them?

Making up her mind that there was no point wasting time wondering what he wanted until she actually heard from him, Lara spent a frustrating morning deliberately doing much-needed chores around the flat—which would give her a legitimate excuse to stay in while not looking as though she was deliberately hanging around waiting for Darian Wildman to ring.

He didn't.

By nine o'clock that evening she was feeling pent-up, frustrated and angry with herself, telling herself that it shouldn't matter. Of course it shouldn't. But Jake had gone to stay with his parents, so she couldn't even drag him out for a pizza, and it was too late to ring anyone else. Instead she had a long, scented bath, taking care to leave the bathroom door open just in case the phone rang. And of course it did, just as she was up to her neck in jasmine-scented bubbles.

Leave it on the machine, she told herself sternly. If he really wants to speak to you he'll ring back.

But she found herself clambering out of the bath, dripping water all over the bathroom floor, and depising herself for doing so.

'Hello?'

'Lara? It's Darian.'

She knew that; he had one of those voices which, once heard, was never forgotten. Briefly she wondered whether to play the game a little and say, Darian *who*? but decided against it. A man like that would be used to the pointless little games that some women played, and he would like her no better for it.

'Hello,' she said.

'I haven't disturbed you?'

There were games and there were games, and half-truths were sometimes necessary—especially if you wanted to avoid looking like a fool.

'Not really.' She watched the water running down her bare legs to form a small puddle on the bathroom floor. 'I was just…relaxing.' Which didn't have even a grain of truth to it, because she had never felt less relaxed in her life. And there seemed something slightly decadent about talking to him while she was naked, so she injected a brisk and professional note into her voice. 'What can I do for you, Darian? Have you seen the photos yet?'

'That's what I've just been doing.' He allowed himself a brief half-smile. It seemed that his instincts had not failed him—because Lara looked nothing short of sensational. Some of London's most stunning backdrops emphasised her bewitching looks as she stood holding a variety of his company's phones in her hand, a dreamy, thoughtful little smile on her face. She looked as if she was talking to her lover. Beneath each one would be printed the single shout-line: *Wildman: Presses All The Right Buttons!*

He had felt the unmistakable tremorings of desire as he had studied them. But, having seen them, had wondered aloud to Scott whether the final images weren't just *too* sexy. Scott had shrugged and given him a knowing look.

'Oh, come on, Darian—you don't use a young and beautiful model to do anything *but* sell sex,' he had pointed out. 'Do you?'

Selling sex.

Put like that, it sounded off-putting, and Darian had grimaced with a slight element of distaste—but that hadn't stopped him finding her number and ringing her, had it?

'They're terrific,' he said softly.

'Good. I'm pleased.' She waited. She knew that she wanted to see him again, in fact she *had* to see him again, but she was perceptive enough to know that she was dealing with a man who would always be pursued, and natural predators did not *like* to be pursued.

'I wondered if you'd like to have dinner with me?' he asked. 'As a kind of thank-you for turning in such a fantastic job.'

Lara very nearly asked him whether he always asked people out to dinner on the strength of their having done a good job, but she knew she couldn't risk scaring him away.

This, after all, was precisely why she had fought to get the job in the first place. To get closer to Darian, to find out as much as she could about him before she told Khalim what she knew.

'I'd love to,' she murmured. 'When?'

Human nature was a funny thing, Darian decided as a contrary feeling of disappointment washed over him. He hadn't expected it to be quite so easy, but why on earth should it make her seem marginally less desirable because she had not played games with him?

Because women always made it this easy for him, that was why. Had he hoped that her spikiness and spirit would make him have to battle for a bit to get her to agree to have dinner with him—and hadn't there been a part of him which had been anticipating that battle?

'I don't suppose you're free tomorrow night?'

Lara heard the slight cooling of his voice and knew

immediately that she had been too eager. 'Not *tomorrow* night, I'm afraid.' She paused, waiting.

Darian relaxed. There was nothing more off-putting than a woman who dropped everything because she wanted to see you—or, worse, a woman who had a social diary with great yawning gaps in it. But then he thought about her sparkling blue eyes and her perfect figure and guessed that Lara Black would not suffer from a lack of anything to do.

'Thursday, I'm flying to Paris for the day,' he mused. 'And I'm back late. How about Friday?'

She paused for just long enough to sound as though she was consulting a diary—after all, he wasn't to know that she was standing dripping in the bathroom, with her body tingling not just from the cold but from the effect of that rich, deep voice and the thought of seeing him again.

Because you *need* to see him, she reminded herself firmly. 'Friday's fine,' she said calmly.

'Shall I pick you up?'

To her horror, she felt her breasts tighten in response to the sudden softening of his voice, and the face which looked back at her through the blurred and misty mirror was startled. And confused. She didn't want to be attracted to him—certainly not *this* attracted. So she'd spend one evening with him, she told herself. That was all. 'Okay,' she said slowly.

'Good. Give me your address, and I'll see you around eight.'

Darian parked the car, expertly edging into the tiny space available at the address she had given him, and as he switched the powerful engine off he registered that he was surprised.

So she lived in Notting Hill, did she?

Which meant that she was successful. Property in this part of West London was astronomically expensive these days, ever since it had become 'the' place to live, with rock stars and Hollywood actresses swooping in to buy up every graceful house available.

Except that no one had heard of Lara Black—not really. So how come all the outward trappings of success? Scott had told him that she had done a few forgettable plays and a couple of television commercials where she had either been playing a vegetable or lost in a crowd of people drinking cola. But she'd been in nothing major to date.

He climbed the elegant steps to the house and pressed the button for Flat B. She probably rented, he reasoned. Or shared with a group of other impecunious women, pooling their resources so that they could live in an area with a prestigious address.

The door opened and Darian's eyes narrowed as he was greeted by a tall man with a lock of hair flopping into his eyes. Darian was rarely taken off-guard, but this time he was—amazed to be staring into the face of a stranger who was instantly recognisable. You would have had to have been living underground not to have recognised the star of the film which had broken all records at the international box-office last year.

What the hell was Jake Haddon doing *here*?

'I'm looking for Lara Black,' growled Darian.

Jake smiled. 'I know you are, but she's having one of those dress crises that women are prone to. The last thing I heard was a squeaked request from the bedroom asking me to answer the door! Come up and have a drink,' he offered easily.

'Thanks,' said Darian shortly.

He followed Jake up the stairs, his mind buzzing. What had Jake said? *A squeaked request from the bedroom.* So what kind of bedroom was that? A *shared* bedroom? And if that were the case then why had she agreed to have dinner with him tonight? Unless she had thought it was business—that he wanted to discuss the shoot with her.

Darian was unprepared for the overwhelming sensation of irritation and—*disappointment*.

He walked into the flat, which was huge—but at least now the up-market address became understandable. Of course she could afford to live in a place like this if Jake Haddon was footing the bill!

'Drink?' asked Jake.

'I'm driving.'

'Something soft, then?'

Darian forced himself to be pleasant, though he most decidedly did not feel it. In fact, he was feeling at a distinct disadvantage—a situation which was both novel and unwelcome.

'No, thanks. I'll just wait for Lara,' he said, and summoned up a brusque smile from somewhere.

'I'd better go and hurry her up, then.'

Darian nodded and watched the actor as he disappeared out of the room with a familiar loping stride. Funny, he thought, how celluloid could make you feel you knew someone—the way they walked and the way they spoke.

There was a tap on the bedroom door. 'Lara?'

Lara looked up. 'Oh, Jake! Come in! Do I look okay?'

'You look gorgeous, darling—but why go to so much trouble to date a man with a face like thunder?'

'Is he cross?' she asked, and flicked a glance at her watch. 'I don't see why—I'm only a couple of minutes late!'

Jake shrugged. 'It might be me—you know the effect I have on boyfriends.'

This was true. 'He isn't a boyfriend,' she protested unconvincingly, and then stared at herself in the mirror. She had chosen a cream silk dress with hundreds of tiny little buttons down the front, worn with black knee-length boots. 'Do I *look* as though I've gone to a lot of trouble?' she moaned.

'As if you've tried on a hundred dresses and then a hundred more? Stop frowning, darling—I'm only teasing—and run along and greet him. I think I'll go and hide in my room in case he decides to take a pop at me!'

Lara's fingers were trembling as she picked up her bag, and her heart was crashing against her chest as she walked into the sitting room to see Darian Wildman studying all her books in the manner of a detective on the lookout for pornographic literature!

He must have heard her, for he turned round as she walked in and she couldn't mistake the inky dilation of his eyes as he saw her. She wondered whether her eyes were doing exactly the same thing, because the sight of him made her knees go weak.

He looked all predator again—the cool and uncluttered clothes doing absolutely nothing to detract from his potent masculinity. His tawny skin gleamed as though it was lit from within and the golden eyes seemed to look at her too long and too hard. Too everything, really, because when he stared at her like that it was difficult to remember that this was not a normal man and this was not a normal evening.

'Hello, Darian,' she said, in a voice which sounded surprisingly calm.

Darian sucked in a breath because she looked utterly…not quite beautiful, because the term implied a set of criteria which needed to be filled and her looks were much too distinctive for that. But she had a definite head-turning quality which was difficult to define. Gorgeous, yes. And sexy, too—in a simple little cream dress which fitted her much too well and high-heeled black boots that made his gaze want to linger on her legs for ever.

Distracted, he broke a lifetime's rule and spoke without thinking of the consequences. 'You didn't tell me you lived with Jake Haddon!' he accused silkily.

And a very good evening to you, too! thought Lara. 'Why on earth should I have done? And, anyway, I don't *live* with him—I share a flat with him!'

Darian had been unaware that he was holding his breath until it was expelled in a long, low rush. Well, that told him something! When a woman said she shared a flat, it usually meant that she *wasn't* sharing a bed. He looked around the room and then back into her eyes. 'Lucky you,' he said softly.

'Or lucky him?' she countered sweetly.

'I should think that ninety-nine per cent of the female population would give anything to trade places with you.'

'Which presumably is why *I'm* sharing a flat with him—since I'm in that incomprehensible one per cent to whom it doesn't really matter that he's a handsome film star—just that he's a very nice person!'

Jealousy was not an emotion that Darian was used to feeling, and he was not enjoying it. With an effort, he glanced around the room, reluctantly acknowledging its style and taste. 'Pretty nice place he's got!'

It was with indignation that Lara opened her mouth to demand how he dared jump to that conclusion—even though it was the obvious one to reach. But to do that would be to tell him that the apartment belonged, in fact, to her—and then she would also feel duty-bound to explain why, and risk arousing his curiosity.

He seemed such a judgemental man that he would probably conclude that she was running an escort agency—or something equally wicked!

'Yes, it's beautiful, isn't it?' she agreed conversationally, because this really was straying into dangerous waters.

The apartment had been given to her by Khalim, after his wedding to Rose. He had been concerned for Lara's welfare, unwilling to see her living in a crummy little place after he whisked her best friend and flatmate off to live in Maraban.

He had handed her a ribbon-tied envelope before he and Rose had flown off for their honeymoon and Lara had waited until they had gone before she opened it.

She'd only ever been a bridesmaid once before, and then she had been given a sweet gold St Christopher to hang around her neck. She had almost fainted with shock to find inside the envelope a set of deeds which showed her to be the owner of the most gorgeous flat she had ever seen!

'I consider myself very lucky,' she said truthfully as she gestured to the high ceilings and the elegant dimensions of the room.

Darian watched her, unable to deny that his interest in her had increased, due as much to her modesty as anything else. Most women would have boasted of their connection to such a high-profile star, not played it down. It was the last thing he had expected, and surprise was such a rare commodity that it would have set his pulses racing.

If they hadn't been racing already.

'Shall we go?' he said evenly. 'My car's outside.'

'Okay.' Only now her voice didn't sound so calm. Could he hear that she was almost breathless with anticipation and apprehension at the thought that they were now to leave the safety net of her home, with Jake lurking comfortably in the background?

Soon she'd be alone with this handsome, exotic stranger in his car, nursing a secret she didn't know how she dared tell him.

# CHAPTER FIVE

DARIAN'S car was predictably powerful, Lara reflected as she climbed into the low seat with an agility which made her grateful she had done all those ballet classes when she was younger. And suddenly she felt as unsure of herself as that young girl had briefly been—out of her depth and scared.

'Where are we going?'

In the semi-darkness Darian gave a grim little half-smile, realising that Lara was not a woman who would be impressed by status for status's sake. Why, Jake Haddon had probably taken her to every single famous restaurant in London!

'It's a surprise,' he murmured softly.

'Oh, good. I like surprises,' she said—because what else could she have said? That being alone in a confined space with him was making her aware of all the wrong things? Like his powerful, brooding presence and long, long legs, which were affecting her on a purely personal level, and being personal was not supposed to be on the agenda. This was not an expedition to discover their compatibility or to acknowledge the bone-melting effect he had on her, but to find out more about him. She half turned in her seat, looking as a passing streetlight flickered golden highlights across the hard, sculpted profile. 'So where do *you* live, Darian?'

He opened his mouth to answer immediately, and this, too, was a new sensation. Normally he played down his home because of its unmistakable luxury, but for once he realised that he didn't have to! 'I have an apartment overlooking the river.'

'Let me guess—big and stark and minimalistic, with huge windows which look out all over London!'

He shot her a sideways glance. 'Are you a mind-reader, or something?'

'You mean I'm right?'

'Yes,' he growled suspiciously. Frighteningly and accurately right. 'How did you know?'

'Because I'm an actress and we're very perceptive, or at least we're supposed to be—it goes with the job!'

'So it was a guess?'

'An informed guess,' she corrected. 'I could tell the kind of place you definitely *wouldn't* live in.'

'Oh?' He changed down a gear as he cut through a backstreet. 'Enlighten me.'

This bit was easy. 'You wouldn't live in a cosy family house,' she said confidently.

'Because?'

'Because you haven't got a family.'

'How do you know that?'

Lara turned her head back to glare straight ahead into the darkness, her heart leaping with something which felt very like fear. That was a factor which hadn't even entered her head. She hadn't considered that he was a married man, and she didn't want to question why the thought of that should upset her quite so much. 'Well, if you *do* have a family, then you shouldn't be in the habit of taking women who might jump to the wrong conclusion out to dinner!' she said crossly.

'And what conclusion would that be?' he murmured.

That this was a date. Lara suddenly realised that she *wanted* it to be a date. Oh, *why* did he have to have a damned connection to Maraban—and when was she going to get around to broaching the subject?

Not yet, she told herself.

Not yet.

'And where else wouldn't I live?' he asked softly, changing the subject back because she seemed to have lapsed into a thoughtful kind of silence.

Lara settled back in her seat, relieved to discover that, like all men, he wanted to talk about himself. And wasn't that good, in the circumstances? 'Nowhere there are lots of houses all the same,' she said firmly. 'And nowhere that's fussy or predictable—the kind of place where people always do the same thing, day in, day out—you know, like catching the train at the same time every morning and washing their car before lunch on Sundays!'

Unseen, he narrowed his eyes. It was uncanny. Disturbing. How had she managed to echo the very thoughts he had had the other day?

Any minute now she would be telling him what colour boxer shorts he was wearing—Darian regretted that thought instantly, as it was met with an answering jerk of desire.

With a small sigh of something like relief, he drew into the parking lot of the restaurant and Lara peered through the window, interested to see where he had chosen. She had been so wrapped up in him that she had barely noticed where they were going, and this was an area of London she realised she didn't know at all. Had she been half expecting him to opt for some glitzy place right in the centre of the city?

Because this was the very opposite. It was a small, unpretentious building with fairy lights strung outside, making tiny blurry rainbows through the misty autumn air, and as she opened the car door she heard the sound of music. It conjured up memories of days when money had been tight, days when people were happy to eat simply because they were hungry, and not because a restaurant was *the* place to be seen. A little sigh escaped from her lips. Nostalgia could be very powerful.

'Where's this?'

In the circumstances, Darian didn't think it pertinent to tell her that it was a small, noisy, family-run Italian restaurant that he had stumbled on by chance years ago. And that, apart from the food, one of its main attributes was that he was never recognised in there by anyone remotely connected to his business life.

Jake Haddon probably took her to places where *he* wouldn't be recognised all the time, he thought, again with that infuriating shaft of something very like jealousy.

The owner and his wife greeted him warmly, and that, too, took Lara by surprise. Had she thought that he would be aloof—one of those men who swanned into places as if they owned them? They were shown to a table in an alcove—private, yet managing to provide a good view of the rest of the restaurant. It was as if they had been saving the nicest table just for him, and that *didn't* surprise her at all.

As they settled into their seats Lara thought that perhaps this was the best way of all of finding out what the real man was. A one-to-one dinner where she could discover as much about him as possible. It would be like taking an inventory.

'You were miles away.'

His voice was a velvet murmur which nudged into her thoughts, and Lara blinked to find the gold eyes trained on her, piercing through her as if the light which shone from them was the precious metal itself. And for a moment she felt uncomfortable, as if what she was doing was somehow furtive. Well, when she stopped to think about it—it *was*. 'W-was I?'

He gave a wry smile. He didn't usually send women off into a trance! 'Drink?'

Lara nodded. 'Please.'

'What?'

'Whatever you're having.'

He raised his eyebrows fractionally and ordered wine. 'Shall I choose what you're eating, too?' he questioned sardonically.

Lara nodded, enjoying the confounded look on his face. 'Please.' She smiled. 'You've obviously eaten here plenty of times before—I'm happy to take your recommendations.'

'Are you always so delightfully acquiescent?' he questioned, in a voice of silky provocation.

Lara didn't react to the not-so-subtle implication. 'Only in matters concerning my stomach,' she said. 'I'll eat whatever is put in front of me.'

'You don't survive on cigarettes and black coffee, then?'

Lara shuddered. 'You're joking!'

He studied her. A small moonstone necklace gleamed against her pale skin, and it took a supreme effort not to be completely distracted by the soft shadows of her cleavage. She wasn't all skin and bones, like a lot of actresses and models.

'How come you stay so slim?' he questioned.

'I only eat when I'm hungry, and I walk wherever possible.'

'Even in London?'

'Especially in London—it's the best way to avoid the traffic and to see the city properly!'

He ordered, waited until red wine had been poured for them, then sat back in his seat, his fingers caressing the deep bowl of the glass.

'So.'

Lara took a mouthful of wine, needing something to help her relax, to take her mind off the fact that his mouth had softened and she was wondering what it would be like to kiss it.

She smiled. 'So.'

'What shall we drink to?' He raised his glass, his eyes questioning. 'The new face of Wildman?'

'Why not?' Her heart was beating very fast as their glasses touched.

'Soon to be emblazoned on posters all over the country,' he mused. 'How does that feel—knowing that your face will be everywhere?'

'I'm not sure,' she said slowly. 'I've never done a poster campaign before.'

'But you've done other kinds of advertising—television, magazines.'

'A bit.'

'And does it feed the ego?'

It was a mocking challenge. A faintly hostile question. 'Not really. Actors are notoriously insecure,' she said, taking another sip of wine. 'Didn't you know that?'

He shrugged. 'That's the theory, but if that's the case, then it strikes me as an odd type of profession to choose.'

'Maybe the two are inseparable. Maybe it's *because* they're insecure and don't feel comfortable in their own skins that they're able to inhabit someone else's so easily.'

The curve of her breasts gleamed softly beneath the cream silk. 'I can't imagine that *you* feel uncomfortable in your own skin,' he observed quietly. 'When you're so very lovely.'

Lara quickly put her glass down before he could see that her hand was shaking. The compliment warmed and yet alarmed her. This wasn't supposed to be happening. Her body was not supposed to be tingling and glowing and basking in his approbation as a cat would contentedly lap up the warm rays of the sun. This was not a date, this was a fact-finding mission, pure and simple.

If she wasn't careful then they would spend the whole time talking about her, or, even worse, his wretched company, and then, before she knew it, the evening would be gone and she might never have this opportunity again.

The waiter came over, and she waited until he had deposited two dishes of steaming prawns before them.

She speared one uninterestedly. 'Anyway,' she said brightly. 'You know something about me, but I know absolutely nothing about you.' Other than that your contained and watchful silence makes me feel as jumpy as a cat on a hot tin roof.

'But I thought that all actresses were self-centred and like nothing better than to talk about themselves?'

'It's very insulting to continue making those sweeping statements.' Lara narrowed her eyes. 'Though I suspect that's why you said it—to try and stop me asking you questions about yourself.'

The golden eyes bored into hers. 'You're very persistent,' he observed.

'I think persistence is an undervalued quality.'

His voice was cool. 'What do you want to know?'

'Where you were born.' She chewed a mouthful of bread, as if she was just thinking the questions up as she went along. 'Where you grew up.'

Darian went very still, his antennae on alert. 'How very curious,' he murmured. 'Why?'

And Lara realised that she wanted to know in spite of everything, that even if she hadn't opened that letter and needed to find out then she still would have *wanted* to find out more about Darian Wildman. He fascinated her; he was an intriguing man. But he was also a perceptive and intelligent man, and doubtless one who was used to women clamouring to know all about him. And if in the process of finding out about him she appeared like one of many, then that was just too bad. 'I'm interested,' she said. 'That's all.'

He twirled the stem of the wine glass between his long fingers. 'Why do women always want a history?'

'Because we like to know what makes people tick.'

'And men don't?'

'Not really. Men are more interested in the here and now—women like to discover how we got to it.'

'Because?'

Now she spoke from the heart. 'Because our history is what defines us all and makes us who we are.'

Darian's senses would usually have been put on alert at the turn the conversation had taken, but he was lulled by the sudden passion in her voice, by the blue fire which sparked from those long-lashed eyes. She was thoughtful and insightful, not what he had been expecting at all, and the unexpectedness coupled with the novelty made his habitual guard slip a little.

'My history isn't a particularly exciting one.'

She heard the brittle note which edged his voice, and part of her wanted to back off. But she couldn't. This wasn't just some prurient interest, some woman on the make, chipping away at the formidable exterior to find out what had made the man beneath. This was serious stuff.

'Isn't that subjective?' she queried. 'Everyone else's past always seems more interesting than your own—just like other people's relationships always seem to be made in heaven. When you're looking from the outside you don't see all the imperfections; you just get an idea of the bigger picture.'

She was right, of course—and her reference to relationships didn't go unnoticed, either.

'There's no man in your life?' he asked suddenly.

Lara stared at him. 'No.'

'Why not?'

'That's a very personal question,' she protested, feeling her cheeks grow pink beneath the piercing scrutiny of his stare.

'You think you have the monopoly on personal questions, do you, Lara?'

'Of course I don't—and the reason there's no man in my life is simply because there isn't.' She threw him a challenging look. 'I don't need a partner to define me!'

'How very refreshing,' he murmured.

Lara's fork chased a piece of rocket round the plate. 'So, where were you born?' she questioned casually.

'London.'

'Big place.'

'Nowhere you've probably ever visited.' He named one of the city's most run-down areas and watched carefully for her response, noting the instinctive little frown which pleated her forehead. 'You're surprised,' he observed.

'Well…' For once in her life she was lost for words. 'I guess I am, a little.'

'Because it's reputed to be the birthplace of gangsters?' His words were dipped in caustic irony. 'Or maybe you think that if someone's born in a place like that then they stay there—is that it?'

She shook her head a little. 'No…no, that's not what I meant at all. It's just difficult to imagine you being…poor, that's all.'

'Is it?' The dark lashes came down to shutter his eyes. He looked like a lion, Lara thought. The way a lion looked when you thought that it was asleep, only to discover that it was garnering all its energy to pounce. Lots of men tried to pounce on her, and usually it made her recoil, but Darian Wildman was a different propositon entirely. The lashes parted again and the golden light from his eyes washed over her.

'For a woman who eats whatever is put in front of her, you aren't managing very well tonight,' he mused.

'I'm not very hungry,' she confessed, wondering if this deliberate change of subject meant that she should now withhold her line of questioning. But somehow the questions no longer seemed important—not when he was looking at her like that.

'Me neither.' He wondered if her lack of appetite was rooted in the same reason as his own. He held her gaze, saw the way her lips parted, and knew that she didn't want to be here any more than he did. He felt another short stab of desire. 'Which makes ordering pudding a complete waste of time, don't you think?'

She nodded, but a feeling of disappointment threatened to well up and spill over. Was he bored and wanting out? Had she overstepped the mark with her intrusive line of questioning? And where did she go from here?

The golden eyes glittered and his dark, lean body was very still. 'Are you tired?'

Lara stared at him as something in his voice told her that the evening was not yet over. Yet the implication behind his question made her tense just as surely as it made her body begin a slow, irresistible flower into life.

This is dangerous, she heard a voice inside her head warning her, but she ignored it. 'Not really,' she said, as though she couldn't care less one way or the other.

'Then why don't we continue this fascinating discussion back at my place? You can enjoy one of the finest views over London while I give you…' He paused, his voice lingering deliberately. *'Coffee.'* The golden eyes glittered, and dazzled her with their precious fire. 'What do you say, Lara?'

It was what they called a loaded question, and the unmistakable air of sensuality he exuded warned her that a wise woman would thank him politely and say no. If lion he was, then why be foolish enough to walk meekly into his den?

But she might not get this chance again, and here he was offering opportunity on a plate. She reassured herself that he was far too sophisticated to do something as crass as leaping on her if she didn't want him to. The only thing she had to fear was the fact that she *did* want him to.

Miraculously, she kept the excited tremor from her voice. 'Sounds good,' she said carefully.

'Then I'll get the bill,' he said, equally carefully, and his eyes narrowed.

For once, he hadn't expected it to be quite so easy.

## CHAPTER SIX

'OH, IT'S beautiful,' said Lara softly. She leaned over the balcony and gazed out. The mist of earlier had cleared, and now the lights of the city sparkled like precious gems against the navy velvet of the night sky. 'Just beautiful.'

Darian eased the cork from a bottle of wine and watched the way the breeze ruffled her dark silken hair, so that it fluttered behind her like a banner. 'Yes,' he agreed slowly.

For once he had been wrong—imagining it would take more than a little persuasion to get her to come back here with him tonight. The prickle of anticipation he had felt—that here was a woman who might make him fight a little—had been replaced by the much more familiar feeling of slightly jaded anticipation, but not jaded enough to stem the rising tide of desire.

'Some wine?' he drawled.

Lara turned round. He had removed his jacket and he looked relaxed, almost domesticated. Behind him, the brightly illuminated room looked like the stage-set of a play, with he the hero of the piece.

Or the villain.

Her heart thudded. 'I thought you promised me coffee?'

'I did. But how about a little wine first? You hardly drank a thing in the restaurant.'

A faintly bored note came into his voice, as if her inference that he was trying to push alcohol on her was offensive.

'But I'll go and make coffee if you'd prefer.'

'No. Actually, I'd love some wine,' she said truthfully. Perhaps wine might make her stop feeling like a woman who had never been invited into a man's home before. She wasn't such an innocent! She crossed her arms over her chest and rubbed them up and down her bare arms. 'Brrrr! It's freezing.'

'Go inside. Make yourself at home.'

She felt his eyes on her as she made her way back into a sitting room which was a byword for luxury. This was crazy, she thought. She had spent her life being watched, sometimes on stage and sometimes by the camera, and usually she managed it with aplomb—easily becoming the person the director wanted her to be.

And maybe that was the problem here—that she was being herself. Only she was discovering an unwelcome and unfamilar nervousness in the company of a man who intrigued and attracted and disturbed her, compounded by what she had read in the letter.

Darian followed her into the room, tipping just a tiny amount of the rich red wine into two crystal glasses while she sat down primly on one of the giant leather sofas.

He noticed the way she pressed her knees tightly together as he handed her the glass. Did she always do this? he wondered. Send out such beguiling and conflicting messages? She had agreed very quickly—too quickly—to come home with him, and there was a not-so-subtle subtext to deals like that. If you didn't want a man to make a pass at you, then you did not go back to his apartment late at night on a first date.

Darian was used to knowing the score. To women quickly and blatantly letting him know that they wanted him. It happened so frequently that it was just par for the course, as natural as breathing for him—he had never had to fight for a woman in his life, though sometimes he had idly wondered what it might be like to have to do so.

He was instinctive enough to know that the attraction between he and Lara was mutual, but only up to a point.

Because now there was a wariness about her, almost a shyness, which seemed to contradict her innate sensuality. And mystery and contradictions were always fascinating, he acknowledged with a slow ache of awareness as he sat down on the sofa—just far enough away not to threaten her, but close enough to smell the soft scent of lilac which drifted from her pale skin. Close enough to touch…

Lara sipped her drink, but her throat felt tight and she had to force down a mouthful of the smooth, rich wine. 'Lovely,' she remarked politely.

'So where were we?' He put his glass down on the coffee table and half turned to look at her, a small smile playing around the edges of his mouth. 'Ah, yes, your tender heart was melting at the thought of my underprivileged upbringing.'

With a shaky hand she put her glass down next to his. 'Don't make fun of me.'

'Is that what I was doing?' he murmured.

'That or patronising me,' she answered quietly. 'You don't have to talk about your childhood if you don't want to.'

Liar! Liar! But her words had exactly the desired effect. By telling him he didn't have to talk, he immediately began to relax—although had she known that on some deep, gut-level? That here was a man who would not be forced into telling anything about himself—and the only way to get information about him was to appear not to care?

'And poor doesn't mean unhappy,' she continued coaxingly.

He gave a low, mocking laugh. 'That's the fairytale version, spoken with the voice of someone who has absolutely no idea what material deprivation is like.'

'You can't know that!' she protested.

'True,' he agreed. 'But I'm right, aren't I?' The golden eyes flickered over her lazily. 'Let me guess—you grew up in the country? A stable family life with brothers and sisters? Fresh air and exercise and three meals a day? A pony in the stable and dogs barking when you came home from school?'

Lara froze, then swallowed, and the tiptoeing of fear began to shiver its way down her spine. 'That's…that's bizarre. Well, except for the brothers bit—I have two sisters and they are much older. And my father was away a lot. But the rest is correct.' Her blue eyes were as big as saucers as she looked at him. 'How could you possibly have known?'

'About the country?' Some things you didn't need to be told. He reached his hand out and lightly touched her cheek. 'It's written all over you. Skin like this wasn't made in a city.'

Was that a trace of wistfulness in his voice, or was she imagining it? 'W-wasn't it?'

'No.' He let one of his fingers drift over skin that felt like satin. 'You're a real milk and honey girl!'

Lara found the compliment shockingly satisfying—almost as gratifying as the all too brief contact when he had touched her, making her want him to touch her again. She shook her head slightly, trying to remember why she was here.

'Very good. Ten out of ten,' she said lightly. 'Your turn now.'

'Isn't this supposed to be a guessing game?' he mocked.

'Well, I know you grew up in the city.' Lara drew a deep breath and decided to go for broke. 'I'd say that you are an only child and that your parents were…separated.'

There was an odd pause. 'Is it really that obvious?' he questioned, and a slightly bitter note came into his voice. 'Do I have one-parent family written all over me?'

Lara felt guilty, but she managed not to show it. 'Not at all,' she said hastily. 'It's more a case of working things out from the information available. Putting bits in, like a jigsaw. The area you mentioned doesn't really conjure up a cosy family scene, with roses round the door.'

'As opposed to the image of a mother who was hard-pressed to put food into her hungry child's mouth?'

'Is that what it was like?' she whispered, horrified.

'Not quite,' he commented sarcastically. 'But I should hate to puncture the little bubble-picture you've invented in your head!'

'Now you *are* making fun of me.'

'I thought that all women liked to be teased?'

He was making her feel gauche and unsophisticated. And she didn't like his constant references to what 'women' liked—it made her feel one in an endless line of them—which, when she stopped to think about it, she probably was. But this isn't about you, Lara, she reminded herself—it's about him. And Maraban. 'But you *were* poor?' she questioned bluntly.

His eyes grew flinty. 'Do you want me to give you a breakdown of our weekly finances?'

She heard the distaste in his voice, and she didn't blame him—her questions were crossing over the line between good taste and bad, and unless she gave him some kind of explanation she couldn't possibly keep on asking them. What on earth was she going to *do*? Tell him, or tell Khalim first?

'You're right. I'm sorry—I was just being nosy. Don't worry, I won't ask any more.'

Darian studied her, noting the way her blue eyes were suddenly looking haunted. The vulnerable little tremor of her lips made him want to kiss them. 'You know, you really are very sweet, Lara,' he said softly.

A pain stabbed at her heart. What would he say if he knew? And how could she suddenly just blurt it out—

Darian, I am almost certain that you are the illegitimate brother of the Sheikh of Maraban?

'I am not sweet,' she contradicted, and bit her lip.

'And so modest, too,' he teased. 'Now, don't frown. Relax.' Casually, he reached out to capture a handful of her hair, and began to trickle his fingers through the silky curls so that they touched and tickled the back of her neck. 'Relax,' he whispered softly.

'Darian, don't,' she said weakly.

A woman didn't cross and uncross her legs in quick succession and then wriggle her head back into your hand if she meant *don't*.

'Don't what?' He moved closer, moved his hands from her neck to her shoulderblades. 'You're tense,' he exclaimed softly, and began to gently massage the tight flesh. 'Very, very tense.'

If only he knew why! 'This…this isn't such a good idea—'

'What isn't? A simple massage? I'm very good at it, you know.' His fingers continued to knead away, lulling her into a dreamy and hypnotic state. 'Relax, Lara—if you don't like it, then I'll stop.'

Which made it even worse. He was giving her a let-out. The decision was completely in her hands. She could stop him whenever she wanted to, and she should stop him now. Except that she *did* like it; that was the trouble. She liked it a lot. It's only a massage, she told herself dreamily.

'Is that good?' he whispered.

Helplessly, she closed her eyes. 'I, oh…yes.' The decision wasn't in her hands at all, she realised—he had all the power.

'Why not lie down?' he suggested. 'You'll be more comfortable that way.'

It was, after all, only a massage. She tried to tell herself that as he was gently pushing her back against the sofa.

But the word 'push' implied force, and there was no force involved—merely a delicious compliance as she sank down onto the leather, her cheek resting on its soft surface, her eyelids fluttering to a close.

Darian worked on her neck and her shoulders, gradually feeling some of the tension released by the rhythmical movement of his fingertips. 'Is that better?'

'It's...heaven,' she mumbled.

It felt pretty good from where he was sitting, too. A little too good. Darian shifted his body slightly as the tightness easing away from her body was replaced by a growing tension in his own.

Lara's limbs felt as fluid as water, her blood as thick as warm honey, and the pulse-points around her body began to deepen and speed. She could feel their slow and relentless pounding in her temple, her wrists, and somewhere deep in her groin. This is sheer craziness, she told herself. But she couldn't move; she didn't want it to end.

He heard her sigh, and his hard mouth glimmered in a brief smile, his eyes drifting over the tight, firm curve of her bottom.

'Am I sending you to sleep?'

'Well, yes,' she murmured drowsily, knowing that was only half the story.

'Then I'd better stop. We can't have that.'

He took his hands away. 'Oh!' Lara whispered disappointedly.

'Turn over,' came the soft command.

Somehow she managed to, even though her body felt so deliciously lethargic that it took all her energy.

Her hair was all mussed, her cheeks pink and flushed, and behind her half-hooded eyelids her blue eyes glittered hectically. He read in them self-doubt and utter confusion and, almost without intending to, dipped his head and brushed a featherlight kiss over her lips, felt her shiver in response.

'Darian—'

'Shh.' He kissed her again.

This was dangerous. The brush of his lips was barely there and then gone again, only to return. Tiny, butterfly kisses which coaxed and maddened. 'Oh,' she murmured instinctively.

His mouth smiled against hers, and this time his lips stayed longer, teasing and caressing until hers opened beneath his and her arms came up to wind around his neck, like tendrils of ivy clinging to sun-warmed brick.

'Darian—'

'You don't like it?'

She grazed her lips over his, unable to stop herself. Just once, she told herself. She would kiss him just once. But she kissed him again, and again, and then again, and his low laugh of delight made her want to do it some more.

She tried to speak, but her lips were so dry and her head so spinning that the words came out as a parched kind of whisper. 'It isn't a question of not liking…'

'But that's the only important question, darling. Nothing else is worth asking.' He drifted his mouth along the line of her jaw. 'Is it?'

Her head fell back and his lips moved immediately to her neck. Lara shuddered. In her befuddled state of desire his words seemed to make perfect sense, and this was dangerous indeed. Very dangerous.

She should pull away and ask him to take her home. If he wanted her that much then he would be prepared to wait—and wouldn't that be what any woman in her right mind would do? Wait at least until she had told him the momentous news she had?

So why were her fingertips running over the back of his head as if learning him by touch? Why was she doing nothing to stop him when he ran the flat of his hand down over one breast and then back again, where it lingered, and she could feel it growing tight and hard against him.

Because she couldn't, that was why.

She lifted her head, which felt as if it was weighted with some heavy metal—like the gold which matched the hot, molten colour of his eyes. Two flares of colour ran along each aristocratic cheekbone, and at that moment he looked like a pure Marabanese, with all the accompanying pride and arrogance that went with that ancestry.

Yet his hard mouth had been softened by her kisses, so that for one second he looked unexpectedly vulnerable. It was like having a curtain twitch and seeing behind it a glimpse of a man you dared not dream existed. A man with softness beneath the hard, polished exterior, making him utterly irresistible. And with something approaching shock Lara realised that she wanted him now, no matter what the consequences.

She remembered the first time she had seen Khalim and had almost melted into a puddle on the floor. Was she just one of those women who were suckers for arrogant and exotic-looking men who seemed to make most normal men look like a pale imitation of the real thing?

Darian sensed her reservations melting away and smiled lazily as he ran his hand down over her stomach, which curved faintly beneath the clinging cream fabric of her dress, and then down further still, until it edged up beneath the thin material. He splayed his fingers with arrogant possession over the space of cool flesh above her stocking top and Lara felt her thighs part, as if no power on earth could have stopped them.

'You *do* like it,' he purred approvingly, and the pad of his thumb stroked the silken flesh there. He felt her squirm, enjoying the look of helpless pleasure which made her lips form a disbelieving little Oh!

She tried one last, futile time. 'We shouldn't be doing this,' she protested half-heartedly.

'Want me to stop?' This as his fingertips floated tantalisingly close to the moist, filmy barrier of her panties, and she shook her head distractedly.

'No!'

He kissed her, and his words were muffled against her lips. 'You just want me to know that you aren't in the habit of leaping into bed on a first date, is that it?'

Lara felt her cheeks grow hot. 'Well, I'm not—'

'And neither am I,' he murmured silkily. 'So we're equal, aren't we?'

If only he knew!

'And now that we've established that…' He pulled her into his arms and began to kiss her—only this time he *really* kissed her, deep, searching seeking kisses, which dissolved away everything but the need to be joined with him.

'Darian,' she moaned weakly as he started to unbutton her dress, little by little, bit by bit, lowering his head so that where his fingers led his mouth followed, annointing her skin with gentle kisses which made her squirm with pleasure. He slipped the dress from her shoulders and it slid away unnoticed, so that she was lying there in a tiny cream bra and knickers, her stockings and black leather boots.

Darian sucked in a hot, ragged breath. Women only ever wore undergarments like that if they were expecting to be seduced. This was what she wanted. What she had obviously expected. The heat built up inside him. 'Undress me,' he urged. 'Take my clothes off, Lara.'

But Lara felt almost kittenish in her helplessness. Her fingers fumbled at the buttons of his shirt until he made a low sound that was halfway between a groan and a laugh and tipped her chin up with his fingertip, unbearably excited by the beguiling contrast beween wanton abandon and a kind of sweet shyness.

'Your hands are shaking,' he said gravely.

Her whole body was shaking—surely he could see that? 'Yes.'

He pulled at his shirt with a hunger so sharp he scarcely recognised it. What invisible buttons was she pressing? he wondered distractedly as he yanked it off and impatiently threw it aside.

She saw the tension on his face and managed to undo his belt, but he unzipped his trousers himself, as though not trusting her to do so. Her lips were parched with both fear and excitement as the last of his clothing was removed, and she gave an instinctive sigh as she feasted her eyes on him.

His body was as beautiful as she had known it would be—his skin the colour of deep honey, his limbs long and lean and strong. And he was very, very aroused...

He ran a slow finger over her leather boot and up along her thigh, and felt her shudder in response. 'Do you want to wrap these round my back?' he whispered.

It was one of those questions which told her exactly what the score was. A deliberate and studied celebration of sensuality and nothing more than that. But Lara was too much in thrall to back out now—and what reason could she possibly give? That she was afraid he was going to hurt her as no man had ever hurt her before nor would again?

Instead, she reached her arms up to pull him close, and as he lowered his body down onto hers she had the strangest feeling of inevitability—as though this moment had been determined from the first time she had set eyes on him, as though her life would somehow be incomplete without this.

'Wait!' he commanded, and reached down to pull a packet of condoms from the pocket of his trousers.

'I'm...I'm on the Pill,' she said, her voice shy, which in itself was madness in view of the intimacy of their naked bodies.

Golden eyes glittered. 'Let's just be sure, shall we?' he murmured, and slid one on.

Lara felt heat suffuse her cheeks. He was only being safe and sensible, the way she would have wanted and expected him to be, but it made her feel as if this was just...mechanical instead of special. Part of her wanted to pull her clothes back on and run away, but he had started to kiss her again, and the sweetness of his lips made flight impossible and unwanted.

'Lara!' Darian groaned as the hard, flat planes of his body met her moist and giving heat, bending his mouth to hers. Their lips met and fused and a strange warmth filled him. What the hell was she *doing*? What game was she playing that could have him feeling like this?

All she was doing was holding him in her arms, her hips rising up as if to invite him inside, and suddenly he knew he could wait no longer.

The last of her doubts fled as she felt him tremble because helplessness in such a strong man could be very potent. 'Yes,' she whispered, as if she had read his mind. 'Oh, yes.' But he was already entering her, plunging deep, deep inside her, and she gasped with delighted pleasure.

He heard the sound she made and felt a wild and exultant kind of joy, steadying himself as he began to move. She moved in harmony with him, and he watched the rapture flower and bloom on her face.

Lara's breath caught in her throat. It had never been like this. Never. So... Her eyes snapped open and she saw the dark and golden man who moved above her with such sweet and piercing precision. How could she be this close? This soon? This…?

'Darian!' It was a sigh and a cry laced with a sense of wonder.

But he was a silent lover. There was no response at all bar the silken touch of his skin and the feel of him moving inside her—the sudden brilliant gleam from his eyes was the only sign that he had heard her. She had to bite back words of passion, because even though they were joined so intimately there were some things you didn't do. And telling a man like Darian that you thought he was the most wonderful lover was one of them. And then she was past thought…past caring…

Holding back until he thought it might kill him, he looked down and watched her until the instinctive and frantic arching of her back set him free. He let his seed spill into her with a spasm of pleasure which seemed to go on and on and on, and when it was over he felt as though she had robbed him of something. Taken something from him which he had not been ready to give.

They lay there, spent, in shuddering silence for a moment or two, and a tiny sigh escaped from her lips.

'Oh, Darian,' she whispered, and, turning her head, she kissed his shoulder. But he didn't move, didn't answer, just lay there like a statue made of flesh and bone and blood—and that was when the doubts came flooding back, startling her out of her post-coital haze, and she closed her eyes in despair.

What had she *done*?

Lara knew that regret was a waste of time emotion, but it washed over her in a great wave, leaving her shivering and cold in its wake. What in God's name had she been thinking of? To have sex with a man so quickly—and not just any man—*this* man. And she still hadn't asked him the most important question of all.

She licked her dry, parched lips. 'Darian?'

Darian gazed at the ceiling. Usually he felt restless, not dazed like this. He would jump up, make coffee, perhaps play a little music. Indulge in physical activity which put a distance between him and a woman, and that was the way he liked it. A bout of sensational sex should be seen in context, as nothing more nor less than just that.

But tonight felt different. His limbs didn't want to move and sleep was tempting his heavy eyes as his heart slowed into a regular pounding beat. It was as if he'd landed in a warm, safe place and didn't want to leave it.

He fought it, and yawned. He would offer to take her home now. It was always the acid-test—how the woman reacted. Like a cool, emotionally independent woman or like a clinging little girl. The moment you let a woman stay the night she started moving in her toothbrush and leaving pairs of panties around the place—marking her territory. Though when he stopped to think about it he wouldn't mind the tiny little scraps of nonsense which Lara wore lying *anywhere*. In fact, he'd preferably like her wearing them, so that he could slowly remove them and…

'Darian?' Lara said again, as she felt him begin to harden against her, and she wondered if he could hear the worry in her voice.

'Mmm?' He had been about to pull her into his arms again, but something in her question, something in her body language made him tense, and instinctively his features became shuttered. 'Yes, Lara?'

She sensed just as much as she saw his mental retreat. It was there in the yawn, the way he hadn't been tender, or kissed the top of her head, or told her that it had been amazing. But there were still things she needed to know. She had allowed herself to be seduced, and in so doing she had momentarily veered off course, but she needed to know one thing above all else.

'How old are you?'

Darian was rarely surprised by a woman, particularly after he had just had sex with her; women tended to be predictable in their reactions to fast physical intimacy—they either acted as if you were about to start choosing the ring, or they started asking unanswerable questions like, Do you still respect me? But this was the last question he had been expecting.

Was it a Why aren't you married yet? kind of question? And would other inevitable questions follow—like why had he never settled down before and didn't he ever want children? The last drop of pleasure evaporated in an instant, like rain splashing onto a sunbaked pavement. 'Thirty-five. Why?'

She felt the walls close in, and it had nothing to do with the odd, cold note which had entered his voice.

Thirty-five!

Which made him exactly the same age as Khalim. Or, rather, it probably made him *older*—because surely Khalim's father would not have had a lover straight after he was married? And the repercussions of *that* just didn't bear thinking about.

Suddenly something which had been almost abstract was brought into harsh and painful reality, and she knew that this was a responsibility too much to bear alone.

She had to tell someone, but it could not be Darian.

Not yet.

She ran her fingertips over his chest, her blood running icy-cold in her veins.

'I think I'd better go home now,' she said.

He only just resisted a sigh of relief. 'Okay,' he agreed. 'I'll get dressed and then I'll drive you.'

'I can get a taxi.'

'I *said* I'd take you,' he said, in a tone which broached no argument.

Lara thought that she would have preferred to take a cab, alone with the reality of what a huge mistake she had just made.

Because the fact that he hadn't tried to talk her out of leaving told its own story.

## CHAPTER SEVEN

THERE was a click on the line and Lara waited, as she had been waiting on and off for the past two days—but of course it was never going to be an easy matter to get through to Prince Khalim of Maraban. Despite the fact that phone lines to the mountain kingdom were notoriously unreliable, and the fact that she counted herself as his friend, Lara was pragmatic enough to realise that no one ever really became close to such a powerful and enigmatic figure. Certainly not close enough to just pick the phone up, get connected immediately and say Hi!

And she still hadn't worked out exactly what she was going to say to him when he finally answered anyway.

'Hello?'

It was unmistakably Khalim's voice—deep, with the slightest accent. And—Lara didn't know whether she was being simply fanciful—didn't its deepness and richness remind her of Darian's voice?

'Khalim?'

'Hello, Lara.'

He sounded wary, and Lara couldn't blame him. He was married to her best friend Rose, and loved her with a fierce and unremitting passion, but he had spent his life being propositioned and pursued by countless other women. Why wouldn't he be suspicious that Lara had decided to contact him in a way which had been specifically meant to exclude Rose?

'I know you're probably wondering why on earth I'm ringing you, and I hardly know how to begin.'

He made no helpful sound. There was merely silence

from the other end of the phone. It would have been better to tell him this face to face—but he was hardly going to jump on a plane to England on her say-so, just as she was hardly likely to fly to Maraban at a moment's notice.

'Khalim, you know I was working at the Embassy while someone was off sick?'

'Yes, of course.'

'Well…well, one morning this…this letter arrived.' Lara began to speak, scarcely knowing what it was that she said, because the words seemed to come tumbling out of their own accord and she realised just how much she must have bottled it all up. It was incredible, but as the story unfolded it began to sound more real. She told him that she had found Darian, and that she had met him, deliberately and blushingly skating over the graphic details of their meeting.

'And that's it, really,' she finished, and the sense of a burden shared gave her a brief feeling of lightness. 'I'm sure that this man Darian Wildman is your half-brother.'

There was a short silence. She could imagine Khalim turning the incredible words over and over in his mind, choosing his own answering words carefully, as he always did—because men like Khalim could not risk misinterpretation, not even by friends.

When he spoke there was no emotion in his voice. 'You cannot be certain of this, Lara.'

'I know. I only know what I've found.' She paused. 'He…he looks like you.'

This time there *was* a reaction.

'But he is half-English, you say?'

'Yes, he is.' Lara closed her eyes as she remembered the golden eyes and the dark and tawny body, that autocratic air and undeniable sense of solitude which Khalim always carried about him, which Darian shared. 'But he is unmistakably related to you,' she finished softly. 'I am convinced of that.'

Khalim said something rapid in Marabanese.

'He could be a clever fraud,' he bit out. 'An impostor.'

'How can he be? He knows nothing of the claim,' argued Lara. 'Nor anything of the letter.'

'You hinted at nothing?'

'Not a thing.'

'Why, Lara?' asked Khalim softly. 'Why did you say nothing to this man of such a momentous discovery?'

'Because…because…' Her words trailed off as she recognised that a kind of betrayal had occurred—but surely an inevitable one? 'Because my first loyalty is to you.'

'Thank you,' he said simply. 'The question is what we do about it now.'

'Some people might ignore it. Throw the letter away and pretend it never happened. Carry on just as before.'

'Could you ignore it, Lara?'

Doubt and uncertainty prevailed. Her body still ached from Darian's lovemaking, her senses were still full of him, her mind unable to banish the image of his hard, mocking mouth softened by her kisses.

'If you asked me to, then I suppose—'

'No!' He cut into her troubled words. 'Your hesitation does you credit. I would not ask you to ignore it, nor could I ignore it myself—for the hand of fate is at work here. Predestination,' he mused. 'Sometimes friend and sometimes foe, but unable to be ignored or avoided. We cannot pretend something has not happened because something has—and because of it—things are for ever changed.'

'Y-yes,' said Lara falteringly, and she felt the strangest feeling of foreboding tiptoeing its way up her spine as she repeated his words. 'For ever changed.'

There was a short silence, and then, unexpectedly, he asked, 'Do you like him, Lara?'

Lara stared straight ahead. 'Like' him? Like did not seem to be a verb that one would apply naturally to a man like Darian Wildman. It seemed much too bland an assessment. And how could she possibly be objective about a man who had been the most wonderful lover she had ever encountered and yet also the most unsatisfactory? But it had only been unsatisfactory from an emotional point of view, and she had only herself to blame. You should not fall headlong into the arms of a man if you could not cope with the fact that he might reject you.

For there had been no word from Darian—not since he had dropped her off at her apartment two nights ago and dropped a perfunctory kiss on her lips that had felt as cold as ice, as different from his hot-blooded kisses when he was making love to her as it was possible to imagine.

*But he wasn't making love to you,* said that same, cruel voice which had been tormenting her non-stop. *He was simply having sex with you.*

'I'll give you a ring,' he had said, but it had sounded casual, and she suspected that he had intended it to do so. He had waited until she was safely inside her front door and then driven off, his powerful car sounding like a fighter jet as it had roared away.

Lara had hoped—like a foolish holder-on to romantic dreams—that perhaps he might have rung her first thing the next morning, told her that it had been beautiful and that he wished he was waking up next to her. Except she suspected that both those things would have been a lie, and something deep down told her that Darian Wildman might be all kinds of things a woman should steer clear of, but dishonest was not one of them. He would speak the truth, she recognised painfully, no matter how much that truth might hurt.

'I hardly know him,' she answered now, and her own honesty had the power to hurt, too.

She still didn't quite believe that she had let him make love to her so quickly. Lara was no prude, but she worked in an industry which was notorious for its fickle sexual values, and up until now she had always fiercely guarded her reputation. Her lovers had been few, and not one of them had lived up to her unrealistically high expectations—until now. But there again never before had she allowed herself to be seduced with such ease, and then to experience such intense and unforgettable pleasure in the arms of a man she barely knew.

So what did that say about *her*? Maybe she was one of those people who could only be physically fulfilled if there was no true and lasting intimacy. Just like Darian, she recognised, with a sudden sinking sense of insight.

'Lara,' said Khalim urgently, 'I will have to meet him.'

'But how? And, more importantly, where?'

'Rose is pregnant,' Khalim said thoughtfully. 'And must not be worried. If Darian were brought out to Maraban—'

'Khalim,' Lara interrupted, completely forgetting that he was not used to being interrupted, 'I don't think you quite understand—he isn't the sort of man who could be brought anywhere, not unless he was in full agreement.' A bit like you, she wanted to add, except that it was glaringly obvious. 'And what are you going to do? Ring him up and mention that you might be related and would he please fly out to Maraban so that you can check him out?'

'Then I will have to come to London,' said Khalim slowly. 'And you must arrange for me to meet him, Lara.'

But how? thought Lara as she slowly put the receiver down.

Especially if she didn't hear from him.

Which was kind of defining her as a self-made victim, surely? She had been intimate with the man—didn't that give her the right to telephone him?

She knew that in situations like this there were subtle

games played between the sexes, and that the man always liked to feel as though he was the one doing the hunting, but wasn't she in danger of forgetting the bigger picture?

This wasn't about her and Darian and a relationship which seemed to have started and ended on his leather sofa—it was about his ancestry, and Khalim's. *She* had been the one to let her emotions get in the way, to fall for him, but none of that was relevant.

That was when she realised that she didn't have his home telephone number, nor even his mobile—which left his business. She was going to have to ring him up at work.

And what if…what if he didn't want to speak to her?

You cross that bridge when you come to it, she told herself, though her heart was beating frantically as she dialled the number and asked his assistant if he was free.

Another click.

'Darian Wildman.'

Her heart began to pound. 'Darian? It's Lara. Lara Black.'

Darian raised his eyebrows fractionally when he heard her voice. He had been thinking about her and deciding when to call her again. In fact, he had been thinking about her a lot. It had been a pretty amazing evening all round, but something about it had made him wary. And so had she.

It had all been too…too easy, in a way. That wasn't unusual, but it had not been what he had instinctively expected from Lara. Something about it had not seemed all it should be, and he couldn't put his finger on what it was. But it seemed that Lara Black was liberated and bold enough to ring *him*.

He gave a faint smile. 'Hello, Lara,' he said smoothly. 'How are you?'

'I'm…' I'm almost spitting with rage at such cavalier treatment after such an intimate evening, if you must know—but you won't know, because I would never give you the pleasure of telling you, and if it weren't for this whole Maraban business I wouldn't ever see or speak to you again, that's how I am.

That was what she *felt* like saying.

'I'm fine,' she murmured instead. She paused, hating the words she knew she must say next and giving him the opportunity to say them first. But he didn't. 'I was wondering whether I could see you.'

Frankly, he was surprised. She was far too lovely to be chasing after men. Yet he could hear some suppressed emotion in her voice and knew he wasn't being fair to her. Nor, he thought, with a sudden aching memory, to himself. 'That would be lovely.' He paused and his voice softened just as his body began to grow hard. 'I enjoyed our evening together very much.'

Lara felt indignant, filled with a sudden sense of impotence that she was having to put herself in the humiliating position of ringing *him*, seeming as if she was desperate to see him. And aren't you? mocked a voice inside her head. Aren't you?

She set her mouth into a determined line. No, she wasn't. She rated pride far more highly than desire, and this incident with Darian had taught her a salutary lesson. Never again would she allow herself to be carried away by the needs of her body, allow herself to believe that they were the clamourings of the heart.

But she had to see him. This wasn't just a boy-meets-girl scenario; it was a whole lot more. She had set into motion a chain of events, and now it had gathered momentum and taken on a life of its own. She had no part in all this now other than to set up a meeting between Darian and Khalim.

'Yes,' she said softly, closing her eyes and imagining that she was playing the part of a sophisticated woman of the world, used to dealing with the fallout from such casual, passionate dalliances. 'I enjoyed it, too.'

He pictured the soft rose-white skin and the sparkling blue eyes, the gentle swell of her breasts, and all his vague misgivings fell by the wayside as he experienced an overpowering urge to see her again. He felt the hot, hard physical jerk of desire.

'So when?' he asked huskily.

She opened her eyes and glanced down at what she had scribbled on a piece of paper. The times and the dates when Khalim could practically and realistically be in London in person. 'Next week?' she questioned. 'Say, Friday?'

Darian's eyes narrowed at her unexpected response. Friday? He hadn't imagined that she would be so upfront as to say tonight, or even tomorrow night—but next *week*?

The instincts of the hunter in him were aroused. 'You can't make it any sooner than that?'

She knew that she was playing this game well—too well, she thought bitterly—and that if she had suggested sooner then a bored note would have entered his arrogant voice.

'I'm afraid I can't,' she said regretfully.

'So where shall we meet?' he demanded.

'Would you like to come to the flat? Say, lunchtime?'

Lunchtime? Maybe she would be alone in the flat, with Jake Haddon away somewhere. A small smile of anticipation curved his lips as he flicked a glance at his diary and saw that he was busy. He scored through the appointments with a single stroke of his pen and added the words 'cancel them' for his secretary. 'Sure,' he said smoothly. 'That sounds okay. About noon?'

'Noon is fine.' Lara swallowed, suddenly feeling assailed by nerves. 'I'll see you then.'

The week passed by in a curious state where time seemed either to be suspended in a state of utter unreality or to pass in a flurry of high-level communication with Maraban. Lara had the letter itself flown out to Khalim, and he acknowledged it in a telephone call, his voice sounding cool and thoughtful.

She half imagined that a small contingent of his armed guard might accompany him, but when the Prince arrived on Friday, just before midday, he was alone. Lara opened the door to him and blinked in surprise.

'No guards?' she questioned softly, once he had greeted her and she had closed the front door.

Khalim gave a brief smile. 'My emissary and two others are waiting outside. They have orders not to disturb us.'

'Would you like tea?' Lara questioned shyly. 'Mint tea?'

Khalim smiled. 'You remembered!'

'How is Rose?' she demanded eagerly.

'Rose is complaining that she is the size of an elephant! And I have photos to show you of my son.' A frown crossed his dark face. 'She does not know that I am seeing you. For if she did she would ask questions for which I do not yet have any answers.'

'Oh,' said Lara.

It seemed all so incongruously suburban. Khalim sitting on her sofa, drinking tea and proudly showing her photos of his wife and son. He was wearing Western regalia—a beautifully cut Italian suit in charcoal-grey, snowy shirt and a silk tie the colour of an emerald—and he looked just as much as ease in it as he did in his flowing garments of soft gleaming gold.

Outwardly, he seemed relaxed, but Lara could see the faint lines which fanned out from the jet-dark eyes. She wondered if he was worried about problems at home or simply about meeting Darian—but it seemed impertinent to ask.

She found herself comparing him to the man she was certain was his half-brother. Darian was taller and broader, his skin not so dark as Khalim's, and his eyes were golden, not black, and yet there was an unmistakable similarity between the two men. You could see it in the firm and unblinking gaze, and in the almost tangible strength of character which emanated from them. What would happen when they met?

She shivered, and Khalim looked at her.

'You are nervous, Lara?'

'A little. Aren't you?'

He shook his head. 'In Maraban we have a saying: Life is like a narrow bridge—the most important thing is not to be afraid.'

'He's...he's the same age as you, you know.'

'And?'

'What if he's older? Won't that make him the legitimate heir?'

'But he is *illegitimate*, Lara,' Khalim reminded her gently. 'If indeed he *is* my brother.'

So he wasn't taking her word for it, realised Lara—but who could blame him when something so important was at stake?

The doorbell rang, and her eyes opened very wide. 'He's here! What shall I do? What shall I say?'

'Bring him to me,' commanded Khalim sternly. 'And do not worry, little one,' he said, his voice gentling a little.

Lara's heart was beating so fast that she could barely breathe as she walked to the front door. And when she opened it her feelings of apprehension only increased.

For Darian was standing there, looking impossibly gorgeous and so tantalisingly touchable. The breeze had ruffled his hair, so that all its gleaming darkness was emphasised, and the soft, dark cashmere sweater provided a perfect foil for the living gold of his eyes and the tawny glow of his skin. His lips were soft, and so were his eyes.

Without a word, he pulled her into his arms and stared down at her. Did he have some crazy, masochistic instinct which might have denied him such exquisite pleasures when they were here for the taking? She was beautiful.

The other night had been beautiful. He wanted her again and he wanted her right now.

'Lara,' he murmured.

She knew what he was about to do, and knew that she ought to stop him, but she was powerless to resist.

He drove his mouth down on hers, like a hungry man who had just seen food. The touch of her lips brought memories of her body crashing back into sweet, sharp focus and he gave a little moan of pleasure.

Instantly Lara felt herself responding to his kiss, her body beginning to ache and to dissolve into a hot, moist heat, and as he tightened his arms around her she could feel his taut, shivering tension which matched her own.

She splayed her fingers over his back, feeling the hard muscle contrasting with the softness of his sweater, and made a little sound of pleasure as his thigh nudged its way between hers. She felt her own thighs part instinctively, a hot flame of desire shooting up her as he ran his fingertips possessively down over her hips.

And Khalim was waiting next door!

She tore her lips away and opened her eyes to him, startled by the look of naked need on his face. 'Darian, we mustn't!'

He gave a low laugh of pleasure. 'Afraid that I'm going to take you here, standing up in your hallway?' He stroked her trembling mouth. 'You'd probably like it if I did. Come to think of it, so would I.' And then he frowned. 'What's the matter, darling—is Jake around?'

His words brought her quickly to her senses, for they were nothing more than an arrogant sexual boast. An acknowledgment of how easily and how quickly he could make her melt in his arms. And, dear Lord—he was right! If Khalim *hadn't* been here then she probably wouldn't have stopped him at all!

She reminded herself that if Khalim were not here, then he wouldn't be here, either.

She shook her head. 'No. Not Jake.'

How did she say it? She didn't want to anger him, because what was about to happen was going to affect him pretty deeply on some fundamental level, and she didn't know how he was going to react.

'I've got someone I want you to meet,' she whispered.

'Oh, Lara, no,' he groaned. 'Not now! What did you do that for?'

'Come with me.'

Aching, Darian had no choice but to follow her, but he was irritated. He didn't want to meet her friends—not at this stage, and certainly not now!

Lara threw the door open and Darian froze, his instincts immediately alerted to the fact that the man who stood beside the huge marble fireplace, his dark face so cool and expressionless, was no ordinary man. And it had nothing to do with the costly clothes he wore—for many men wore those.

No, it was something in his eyes and in his posture, something which transcended the mundane and the everyday—he wore an air of comfortable superiority, which silently sizzled out across the room and struck an answering chord in Darian himself.

Darian narrowed his eyes, knowing somehow that conventional conversation was both irrelevant and inappropriate. 'Who *are* you?' he demanded softly.

There was a silence which seemed to go on and on. Lara looked at Khalim and saw him give an odd, brittle kind of smile which was tinged with a sadness.

'I am Prince Khalim of Maraban,' he said slowly. 'And I believe that you are my brother.'

# CHAPTER EIGHT

DARIAN kept his face poker-straight, not a flicker of emotion crossing his features. He had always been a past-master at keeping his feelings hidden. As a child he had learnt not to react, and it had stood him in good stead through his life.

He let his mind assimiliate the incredible words that the man had just spoken, then gave a brief, dismissive smile.

'You are mistaken,' he said flatly. 'I have no brother. I have no living relatives at all. Explain yourself.'

Lara gasped, shocked—and so, judging by the look on Khalim's face, was he. She doubted whether he had ever been spoken to like that in his life—except perhaps by his wife, but that was different.

Khalim gave a small nod, as though an unasked question had just been answered, and gestured towards a chair. 'Should we perhaps sit down?'

Darian shook his head, and then slowly turned his head and looked at Lara. For the first time it dawned on him that this man was in *her* apartment. He glanced at the way she stood there, so wide-eyed and expectant and...yes, there was definitely an air of apprehension about her. What the hell was going on?

But Lara was a distraction. He concentrated instead on one overriding fact, and that was the claim which had just been made.

'I think I would prefer to stand.' He looked at this man Khalim, and a vague memory of something he had once heard on the news came drifting into his memory.

A country. Where had he said? Maraban? Yes. Maraban.

'You are the Sheikh of Maraban?' he questioned.

Khalim nodded. 'I am.'

'And why are you here?' asked Darian quietly.

'Because a letter arrived recently at my Embassy in London—a letter from a woman purporting to be your mother—'

'The woman's name?' snapped Darian.

'Joanna Wildman.'

Darian's eyes narrowed and he felt the sudden acceleration of his heart. 'That was my mother's name.' His voice sounded like grit being poured onto melting snow. 'Let me see the letter.'

It was a definite command, thought Lara, wondering how Khalim would react. But he simply nodded as he withdrew the letter from the breast pocket of his suit, almost as though he had been anticipating this request.

Darian's eyes scoured over it disbelievingly, but there was no doubt that the words were written in his mother's hand. 'She died two years ago,' he said slowly.

'Yes. As you will read, the letter was not intended to be opened during her lifetime.' Khalim's black eyes glittered. 'And, as you will also read, she claims that my late father, Makim, was indeed *your* father, too.'

His eyebrows were elevated in question, and the statement he had made was so utterly bizarre that Darian wondered if perhaps he was in the middle of one of those dreams which were so real that you mistook them for reality. Maybe in a minute he would wake up.

But even as he answered he was aware of the first glimmerings of unease. 'I know nothing of my father. Absolutely nothing.'

'No.' Khalim paused for a moment. 'Your mother was an air stewardess?'

'Up until I was born.' Darian's mouth twisted in derision. There had been no mention of her employment in the letter. 'You've had me checked out!' he accused softly.

Khalim nodded. 'But of course.' He paused. 'She flew to the Middle East regularly.'

And the missing piece of the jigsaw which had always eluded him began to hover tantalisingly over the gap in Darian's memory. His mother had spoken of his father maybe once, perhaps twice. He had been a good man, she had said, but a man who was not free and was certainly not in a position to support them. Darian had assumed that his father was married, had noted his mother's reluctance to talk about him and her distress whenever the subject was brought up.

Children soon learnt to make life easy for themselves. When to pry and when to leave well alone. He had accepted her reticence, just as he had accepted that he looked different from the other children. Darian had been focused on the future, on getting out of the poverty of his upbringing. Whoever his father had been he was not a real figure, not in terms of having any influence in his life, and so Darian had simply closed the door on all his questions.

There had been nothing about him in the papers his mother had left after her death, though at the time it had crossed his mind that now he was in a position to seek out his father without causing his mother distress. But Darian had decided to let sleeping dogs lie, asking himself what end it would serve if he went on such a quest—other than to unsettle him. Why pursue a man who had never felt the need to know his son?

But now the past had been dropped before his eyes, falling like a heavy pebble into a pond, its ripple-like effects spreading down through the ages—and for the first time a very important question *did* occur to him.

He turned again to look at Lara, where she stood as still

and as frozen as a statue. 'So what does Lara have to do with all this?'

She had been wondering when he would get around to asking. Lara spoke before Khalim had the chance to defend her. She would not shrink from the truth, not any more.

'I was the one who first read the letter,' she said quietly. 'I was working at the Embassy at the time and it came into my hands.'

'When?'

She heard the raw anger in that one stark word, and flinched. 'Almost a month ago.'

A different jigsaw now, and these pieces slotted into place with insulting ease. He looked directly into her blue eyes and gold accusation flooded over her in a hot, sizzling shower. 'You came looking for me,' he seethed slowly.

'Yes.'

'You chased the job as the face of Wildman.' His dark lashes shuttered by a fraction. 'Didn't you?'

'Yes.'

The lashes moved again, and now there was an odd expression in the strange and beautiful eyes, the cold, cruel smile which glittered over her. She knew what the next accusation would be almost before he had a chance to form the words, and her gaze begged him not to ask it—not here and now and in front of Khalim. But he ignored the silent plea, his voice taking on a bitter, hard timbre she had never heard before.

'Is that why you slept with me, Lara?'

Lara glanced at Khalim, who was observing and listening to the fraught interrogation session in interested silence. Only the faintest elevation of his eyebrows indicated that he had registered Darian's final damning question, but Lara knew that Marabanese men knew the value of silence. He would not interfere in something which did not concern him. She was on her own here.

'I don't think that now is an appropriate time to discuss this—'

'Oh, *don't* you?' His sarcastic words sliced through her half-formed sentence like a knife through butter. 'I don't really think that you're fit to be the judge of what is or is not *appropriate*, Lara!'

He remembered the way her vulnerable blue eyes had made him soften and melt, and then made love to her in a way which had blown his mind, and he cursed silently at his blind stupidity. Of *course* she would be adept at pulling heartstrings—she would know every trick in the book, about how to behave and how to manipulate. She was a god damned *actress*, wasn't she?

He sucked in a deep breath. His rage and his retribution with her could wait. He turned his head towards Khalim again.

'So why are you here?'

'To see you,' said Khalim simply. 'To see whether it was true.'

'But you can't, can you?' drawled Darian. 'You can't tell just by looking?'

'Oh, yes, I can,' demurred Khalim quietly. 'I saw it as soon as you entered the room today. You have the blood of a true Marabanesh running in your veins.'

Something in the way he said it made a small shiver of something unknown snake its way down Darian's spine. Not fear—no, he had never felt fear, nor would he ever give in to the false and futile pressure of fear. Something else—something which momentarily made him feel as if things were edging out of his control. But he deliberately blocked the feeling, substituting it instead with the strength and single-mindedness for which he was known.

'Even if I have—so what?' he challenged, in a low, deep voice. 'It doesn't change my life—how can it? So do not worry, Sheikh—the secret will remain just that. You can go back to your kingdom safe in the knowledge that my life is fulfilled and complete. I have no need of your wealth or power and I will make no claim on it. I give you my word.'

Khalim's eyes narrowed into icy black shards. 'You have no wish to see Maraban?' he demanded, as if Darian had raised a fist and hit him.

Again that tantalising feeling. As if some scarcely heard and hypnotic music were luring him to run away and dance. Darian shook his head, furious with himself for such a bizarre flight of fancy.

'You must come as my guest,' continued Khalim.

The two men stared at one another.

'Why?' demanded Darian simply.

Lara thought again how peculiar it was to have Khalim spoken to like that, and for him to accept it.

'I should like to get to know you better,' answered Khalim. 'Man of my blood.'

If Darian had heard a statement like that even an hour ago he would have given a sardonic laugh. It was not the kind of thing men said to one another—not in his world. But something had inexplicably changed. This whole crazy and bizarre situation was linked to a past of which he knew nothing, and it was that fact which troubled him.

His past.

But the past held no interest for him, he reminded himself. Life lay with the present and the future. His life was here, and it was good.

He shook his head. 'No. I can't see the point.'

Khalim smiled then. 'Can't you?' he questioned softly. 'Can you just let me walk away today, Darian, and turn your back on the opportunity I am offering you? To discover Maraban and in so doing perhaps discover a little of yourself?'

It was a tantalising proposition, and Darian felt the hard,

pounding beat of excitement. He was not into the 'self-discovery' so popular in the modern world. He considered such things an indulgent waste of time. And yet…

Would he be left with a whispering feeling of regret if he turned this opportunity down? He turned his head slowly to look once again at Lara. Her face was pale now, all the roses fled. All he could see were the twin sapphires of her eyes, sparkling blue but wary, almost afraid.

And afraid you should be, he thought grimly.

His lips curved into another slow, cruel smile as a plan began to form in his head, and he nodded. 'Very well,' he said slowly. 'I will accompany you to Maraban—but on one condition.'

There was silence. And when Khalim spoke it was as soft as the hiss of a snake. 'You dare to stipulate a condition?' he demanded. 'Of *me*?'

'If I am your brother—or half-brother,' retorted Darian, 'then some kind of equality must exist. I am neither your subject nor your inferior—am I, Khalim?'

'No,' answered Khalim, and a reluctant smile nudged at his lips as he looked at the man with the golden eyes and the tawny skin. 'Then name your condition, and if it is within my power it shall be met.'

Darian savoured the moment as his eyes captured hers and held them, hard. 'I want Lara to accompany me.'

Khalim nodded, as if he understood perfectly, and turned also to look at her, a silent question stilling the dark features.

Lara's heart pounded with something very like fear. She loved Maraban, and in any other circumstances she would have been overjoyed to be given the opportunity to go there again. But these circumstances were different. She knew without being told that Darian Wildman was not asking her to go with him because he still thought that she was 'sweet' or because he enjoyed her company so much he couldn't bear to be without it.

No, the sudden hardness which had made the golden eyes look so cold filled her with a foreboding that made her skin grow chill, and in that moment she wished she could just close her eyes and be a million miles away from here, and then return to find that none of it had ever happened…

But it had happened.

And didn't she owe it to him—in some strange kind of way—for the way that she had deceived him? And to Khalim, too—who had been so generous to her in the past?

If Darian visiting Maraban was all down to whether or not she would go with him, then how could she possibly refuse?

Her skin felt icy-cold as she nodded, lowering her lashes so that she didn't have to meet that mocking gold stare. 'If that is what you want, then I will comply.' Comply! She sounded like some little subordinate now! Lifting her chin, she turned to Khalim, trying to keep her voice steady. 'Wh—when did you anticipate us leaving?'

Khalim smiled. 'My jet is on the runway. We will leave for Maraban just as soon as you have both packed sufficient for your needs.'

# CHAPTER NINE

DARIAN sat back against the leather seat of the car as it silently and powerfully sped towards the airfield, his mind spinning with thoughts which seemed just too incredible to be true.

Beside him sat Khalim, and in the front, next to the driver, a burly man whose bulk made his position as bodyguard to the Sheikh unmistakable.

Lara had elected to travel in the second car, hastily reassuring Khalim that she would be happy to do so. I bet she is, thought Darian grimly. Deceiving and conniving little Mata Hari! He had read of women who used their sexuality to try to get close to a man, to sensuously make them let their guard down before blowing their lives into smithereens, but he had foolishly imagined that kind of woman to have no place in the contemporary world.

How very wrong he had been!

He felt the jab of fury combined with the hot thrust of lust, but he steadfastly put all thoughts of Miss Lara Black out of his mind. She wasn't going anywhere—or at least nowhere that he wasn't going—and he would deal with her when the time was right. For now, his head was too full of thoughts which sounded more like the plot for some fantastic story. But facts were facts—however incredible—and this was no story, it was his life.

He was going to Maraban! To a mountain kingdom to which, it seemed, he was linked by birth. And through all his anger and confusion he felt the stir of something within him, some soft blaze of an emotion he did not recognise.

He turned to look at Khalim, who had been sitting silently at his side, managing to be both alert and yet relaxed—as though there was little in this world which surprised him, and maybe there wasn't. For wouldn't life as ruler of a country such as Maraban present all kinds of dilemmas and problems which a normal man would never encounter in his lifetime?

'You don't seem angry,' observed Darian quietly.

Khalim turned to him, a wry look on his dark and shadowed face. 'Why would I waste my time being angry about what exists?' he murmured. 'That would be like being angry because it was raining, or because…' He seemed to search for some analogy which the Western man would understand. 'Because the horse you had placed your last dollar on had broken its leg before the big race!'

For the first time Darian smiled. 'I am not a betting man.'

'No? You do not gamble on luck and on fortune?'

'I don't gamble on anything.' And it was true. Gambling was precarious, and Darian had spent his life avoiding the precarious. He made things certain wherever it was possible, and for that you needed something far more tangible than luck. Simple, really. If you worked hard and used all your brains and initiative and imagination then you would reap the benefit of that.

Yet Khalim possessed untold, almost unimaginable wealth, Darian acknowledged as he glanced around the car. This vehicle was bullet-proofed, he recognised, and modified for the man it carried—as different from even a rich man's car as cheap plonk was from vintage champagne.

'We're here,' said Khalim shortly, as the car pulled into the airfield, and Darian saw a gleaming jet sitting there, the tiny emblem of a small flag on its tail golden and rose-pink and a deep sapphire-blue. Blue, like her eyes, he thought bitterly. Like her lying and cheating eyes.

Lara stepped out of the other car, seeing the two tall,

dark figures emerge. Already she felt an outsider—she, who had known Khalim for years now, felt peculiarly isolated as she saw the two men standing together. As if they belonged and she didn't. Or was that just her imagination working overtime, as usual?

But then Darian turned to look at her, and she felt her heart sink. How could such a warm and rich and vibrant colour as gold be transmuted into something so cold and threatening? But gold *was* like that, she reminded herself. The colour was warm, but the metal itself was cold—and since time had begun men had died in the pursuit of the costly and elusive treasure.

She shivered, hugging her coat tightly around her, though she knew that the garment would be redundant once they were in the soft, scented heat of Maraban.

As she stared back at Darian, a wave of longing and regret washed over her. Except that she had nothing to regret, did she? Not really—for the man she yearned for was nothing more than an idealised figment of her imagination. True, he had been passion personified…until afterwards… Remember *that*, she told herself fiercely. Afterwards he had been as cold as the gold of his eyes.

She had lost nothing because there had been nothing between them to lose, other than a brief and beautiful encounter on his leather sofa. A man who respected you and had feelings for you did not take you straight home after such an encounter and then not bother ringing you!

Darian was smiling at her now, but it didn't seem like a smile at all—more like a grim declaration of intent to pay her back for what he undoubtedly saw as her deceit and betrayal.

And Lara had a pretty good idea of how he was intending to extract that payment.

Well, tough, she thought, with a defiant return of some of her fighting spirit. If you think you're going to repeat that physically satisfying but ultimately soulless encounter, then you can think again, Mr Half-Brother-to-the-Sheikh.

So why was it that her stupid heart ached with sadness for what might have been?

Yet the reminder of his cavalier behaviour made her feel better in some perverse kind of way, and she even managed to flash a friendly smile at him as they made their way up the wind-buffeted steps to the aeroplane, only to be met with a tight-lipped glower in return.

The flight was long, but supremely comfortable, and Lara unexpectedly found her eyelashes fluttering to a close. Oh, thank heavens, she thought muzzily as she drifted off to sleep. The last thing she could have endured was Darian's simmering disapproval for six hours!

Darian watched her, saw the way her breasts rose and fell, outlined by the soft pink silk dress that she had changed into. She had been wearing jeans and a tee-shirt, but once the decision to fly to Maraban had been made she had opted for flowing, flattering, more feminine clothes—and she seemed to look at home in them, even here on the aircraft.

He glanced around him. He had flown by private jet a couple of times in his life, but nothing to match this; this aircraft was a curious mixture of the very modern and the very old.

Inside the state-of-the-art plane there were lavish silken cushions to recline on, and mint tea and and sparkling water flavoured subtly with oranges was brought to them by two very beautiful stewardesses who were unmistakably Western.

Khalim waved his hand towards the proffered tray. 'You would prefer whisky, perhaps? Or wine? My culture forbids the use of alcohol, but you are my guest and you must choose what you will.'

Darian shook his head. 'No, thanks. I never drink when I'm flying, and I've made it a rule always to follow the customs of wherever I happen to be.'

'When in Rome?' Khalim laughed softly.

Darian laughed back. 'Or when in Maraban, in this case!'

The joke broke some of the tension and an air of ease settled down between the two men.

The blonde stewardess offered Darian a small dish of pistachio nuts.

'Thanks,' he murmured as he took a couple, automatically registering the sideways glance she gave him, and the way that her uniform clung to her tight and luscious curves.

As she wiggled her way out of the cabin Khalim turned to him. 'She is very beautiful, yes?'

'Very.'

'Her name is Anastasia. You would like to meet her later? When we land?'

Angrily, Darian crushed the empty shells between his fingers. 'You offer women to your guests as you would a dish of nuts?' he demanded. 'Is that another of your customs?' His voice lowered to a hiss. 'Is that what your father did to my mother?'

Khalim appeared unperturbed by his reaction. 'I can assure you that Anastasia has a mind of her own, and would never deign to be offered as you would a bowl of nuts. But she is young and healthy and beautiful—is there such a crime in introducing a woman like that to a man like you? She is a strong woman.' He paused. 'Was your mother not similarly strong?'

Darian nodded. It was not his way to discuss such matters, but this was an extraordinary situation, and for some reason he found himself answering Khalim, wondering if he had been deliberately provoked by him into doing so.

'Yes, she was strong,' he said. 'Necessity made it so.' Hard and proud and strong. Her remarkable beauty had made men flock to her, like moths to a flame, but she had rebuffed them almost coldly, as though she would never again allow herself to fall for a man.

But how deeply had she fallen for Khalim's father? Had it simply been a one-off? A brief passion with unexpected and unwanted consequences? And even if there was any way of ever discovering the truth did he really want to know—or was it better to let things lie?

His golden eyes grew flinty as he gazed into the unfathomable stare of the man who it seemed was his relative, the only person connected by blood to him in the whole world.

'So was that just some kind of crude test?' he questioned softly. 'To set me up with the stewardess? Or merely an attempt on your part to get me to talk about my mother?'

Khalim shook his head, and now his expression looked pained. 'Never a crude test, Darian,' he said sincerely. 'Though perhaps subconsciously I did wish you to speak of your mother. But my primary motive was altogether more straightforward than that. I know the appetites of men, and by your lack of interest it would appear that your appetite has already been satisfied.' He flickered a glance over at the sleeping Lara. 'By Lara,' he said softly.

Darian saw the direction of his gaze and again experienced that potent cocktail of rage and lust. He knew what Khalim wanted to know. Lara was his friend, and he would automatically wish to protect her. But it was none of Khalim's damned business what went on between him and Lara! He would give him the bare facts, nothing more. 'Yes, by Lara,' he said shortly, hastily averting his eyes from her moving silk-covered breasts.

'You are lovers,' Khalim observed.

'Yes.'

'And it is serious?'

'She lied to me,' answered Darian stonily.

'She lied because she was trying to protect me.'

But in so doing she had betrayed him. Surely Khalim could see that? 'Perhaps.'

'You didn't answer my question,' persisted Khalim softly. 'I asked you whether it was serious.'

Darian gave a lazy non-committal smile. 'I don't do *serious*,' he said truthfully.

Through the light mists of her snatched cat-nap, Darian's words came drifting into her subconscious, and as she allowed them to register Lara was filled with a sick, cold feeling. Had he said that deliberately—hoping that she would hear, and hear very clearly in just which category he had placed her? And wasn't it better to know, to hear the truth that she had instinctively guessed at spoken out loud?

She pretended to sleep, but in reality she was listening to their conversation. Darian did not come out with any more comments like the preceding one. Instead, he asked Khalim questions about Maraban, and Khalim began describing the history and the culture of his people, his rich voice softening with innate pride. Now and then Darian prompted him with an insightful question, and once he made Khalim laugh. Lara didn't know why this should surprise her so much, but it did.

Until she reminded herself that Khalim was intimate with few; his position as leader isolated him from confidences and shared jokes.

After a while she made a great show of stirring, and when she opened her eyes it was to find that unforgiving gold stare trained on her. She found herself in the infuriating position of half wanting to go over and slap him and half wanting him to come over and kiss her.

Just reaction, she told herself. He could not be faulted

as a lover, and her body was simply reminding her of that—it didn't mean she had to act on it. She yawned, and the two men turned towards her, but all Lara could see was that burning golden gaze.

Khalim smiled. 'You are rested now, Lara?'

'Thank you. Yes.'

'You will have some refreshment? You have eaten nothing.'

Lara shook her head. 'Thank you, Khalim, but, no. I am not hungry.' She glanced down at her watch. Not long to go now. 'When do we land at Dar-gar?'

Khalim hesitated. 'We are not going to Dar-gar.'

Lara frowned. 'Oh?'

'I am flying us to the western province instead,' he said smoothly. 'To Suhayb.' He saw her look of consternation and his voice softened. 'Rose is pregnant, as you know,' he explained gently. 'And such an unresolved development as this would merely trouble her. I am needed in Suhayb, and it is as good a place as any in Maraban for Darian to see a little of how we live.'

Lara nodded. She had heard of Suhayb, of course, which was Maraban's second city. Rose often wrote long and chatty letters about the country so that Lara felt she knew it well. She was aware that a second palace was sited there, and that the region was fringed by beautiful mountains from which crystal streams flowed to bring life to the parched earth.

'Sounds wonderful,' she said.

As if this was some kind of damned holiday she had booked, thought Darian furiously—until he was forced to remember that she was here solely at his behest! But then the engines of the plane changed sound, giving the signal that they were about to land, and he leaned over to look out of the window, his heart beating with an odd kind of excitement as he stared down into Maraban.

Beneath he could see mountains, snow-capped and gleaming in the late-afternoon sun, so that they looked as if they were lit from within by a copper-red flame. As the plane descended he could see the silver glint of water. His first impression was a land of light and fire. It looked, he thought, like a picture from a child's book.

A child's book. Like the kind he had chosen to escape into, to blot out some of the harsh reality of his upbringing. His mouth hardened as the plane touched down. How different his life would have been if his father had stood by his mother!

Lara stood up and saw his face, and suddenly and inexplicably she felt nervous.

'The cars are waiting on the runway,' said Khalim. 'They will drive us to the palace.'

## CHAPTER TEN

THE palace at Suhayb stood in an oasis of green as verdant and as manicured as the garden of a large English country house. Bright flowers, mainly roses, mingled in riotous and scented glory, and in the centre of a large square space of water a fountain sprinkled, catching the light in rainbow rays, the sound soft and soothing against the occasional cry of some unseen and unknown bird.

The palace itself was fashioned from mosaic in every shade of blue imaginable—from pale sky to deep ocean and a hundred shades in between—and Darian was reminded with an unwelcome pang of how the blueness of Lara's eyes had impressed itself on him the very first time he had seen her.

Damn! He didn't want to remember that—he didn't want to remember anything other than the way she had deceived him.

But as Lara gazed in wonder at the palace all she saw was the gold, which picked out the varying shades of blue, as deep and as rich a gold as the eyes of the man who walked slightly ahead of her beside Khalim, their voices speaking in a low tone, so that she didn't have a clue what they were saying.

Khalim turned, the dying embers of the sun beating down on his head, and Darian turned also, in a disturbing mirror image of the Sheikh. Despite the cool linen trousers he wore, and the fine shirt which hinted at the lean, muscular torso beneath, he looked…

Lara swallowed.

He looked as if he *belonged* here—and she didn't, she

thought, with a slight touch of hysteria. But wasn't that what he was intending her to feel? With that stern and icy demeanour and the cold look of distaste? Didn't he want to make her feel an outsider? To marginalise and isolate her? And you would not need to be a genius to work out why he should wish to do that…

A veiled female servant stepped silently out from the shadows of the magnificent entrance hall and Khalim smiled.

'Latifah will show you to your room, Lara,' he said. 'And Darian will accompany me. You will find there all you need, and later someone will come to collect you for dinner. Is that to your satisfaction?'

What could she say? That she felt as though she was being edged aside, cast in a secondary role by these two powerful blood-brothers? And wasn't it ever thus in Maraban? The men ruled and dominated—certainly in the external world, outside their homes.

Rose at least had the protection of being married, surrounded by the invisible aura which was part and parcel of being loved so fiercely by the Sheikh.

But what was Lara? A second-class citizen who could not even draw comfort from speaking to her friend, pregnant and far away in the capital of Dar-gar. Commanded here by Darian and not knowing his motives—though having a pretty good idea, she thought, with a sudden leap of her heart.

She smiled at Khalim, determined that neither man should see her spirits flagging. She was tired; that was all.

'That sounds perfect,' she said softly. 'I will see you later at dinner.' And she inclined her head very slightly towards the Sheikh.

Latifah led the way through a maze of dark, cool corridors, and when they reached her room she asked Lara in shy, faltering English whether she would like a bath drawn.

But Lara, still reeling slightly from the impact of the lavish suite which she had been shown into, shook her head and smiled.

'I can manage,' she said. 'Honestly, I'm used to doing that kind of thing for myself,' she added gently, as the girl began to protest.

Once she was alone she looked around her—at the arched high ceiling, inlaid with gold, and the leather-bound books which completely lined one wall, beneath which stood an antique and very beautiful writing desk.

It was incredible—like being on the film-set of some lavish epic. The suite was all heavily embroidered drapes and hangings in the richest and most royal of colours. Gold and scarlet, cobalt and jade. The room was thick with the scent of roses which drifted from a copper bowl—all creamy-white and edged with apricot—and Lara touched one of the velvety petals, a shiver running up her spine as she did so.

What was it about this place that seemed to make the senses come to life in a way they never quite did back in England? The room looked so stunningly opulent, and the roses seemed more fragrant than any she had ever smelt before. Through the half-open shutters a warm breeze ruffled her hair like the fingers of a lover, and she closed her eyes, trying to put it all into perspective.

Was it just that Maraban was a world away from her normal life? A world free from pollution and care and worries? At least, it certainly was here—in this isolated and splendid palace.

But there were worries waiting to rear their heads, and the main one was Darian, who had scarcely spoken a word to her since they had left London. All she had been aware of whenever she looked at him was a sensual, smouldering intent that excited her even as it terrified her.

But she ran herself a bath, determined not to fall into

the trap of thinking that just because they were here—and just because of the discovery of his royal blood—he was in some way her superior. He was not. He was her equal, no matter what.

Actually, the bath was more like a mini-swimming pool, she realised with a small sigh of pleasure as she lowered her body into the warm, sudsy water and sniffed at the steamy fragrance of patchouli and sandalwood which filled the air.

Aware that she was indeed very tired, she did not dare soak for too long for fear that she might fall asleep, but she washed her hair, noting that all the luxury beauty products were exclusively French and that it felt like sheer indulgence to use them. It was like being in the most gorgeous hotel, only better.

She had just wrapped herself in a thick towelling robe, and was rubbing at the damp tendrils of her curls, when she heard the sound of a door opening and then closing again. She frowned, standing dead still and thinking that she must have imagined it.

But she had not imagined it. She felt the unmistakable sense of a presence in the adjoining room, and her heart began to pound strong and loud and fast.

She would not run away. She would confront her fear—except that it was not strictly accurate to define it as fear. Not when she knew almost certainly the identity of the person who was moving around. And there was no way she was ever going to be frightened of *him*.

She walked into the bedroom and there, leaning against the shuttered window, his thumbs looped arrogantly in the belt of his trousers, as if he had every right to be there, in *her* room, was Darian.

Lara opened her mouth to speak, and never had speaking seemed such an effort. 'What the hell are you doing in here?'

He gave a smile, the kind of smile which a cobra would probably give if it could, just before it devoured a small animal—whole.

'I'm just waiting for your towel to fall,' he drawled, running his eyes over her with a look of smoky anticipation. 'To see you in all your pink and white nakedness, with little droplets of water still clinging to your soft skin. I would lick them off with my tongue. Every one,' he finished on a murmur, and his tongue snaked out as if to illustrate his words—if any illustration was needed.

Lara tried to look outraged, but the reality was that her body was betraying her sense of shock and debilitating sensual awareness as she imagined him doing just that. Beneath the towel she felt the prickling of her nipples, budding and pointing almost painfully in response to his words. Even worse was the honeyed rush right at the very cradle of her, and she found herself squeezing her thighs together—the way you were taught to in an exercise class. But, oh, what a long way away the gym seemed right at this moment!

'Get out,' she whispered.

He laughed, but it was a cruel, cold laugh.

'You don't want me to go anywhere, you lying little bitch,' he taunted.

She recoiled from his harsh words as if he had struck her. 'Yes, I do.'

'Oh, no.' His voice became a caress of silk and of velvet. 'You want me. You want me to touch you.'

'You're mad!'

He nodded. 'Quite probably,' he mused. 'I must have been mad to have wondered why you were so deliciously compliant on our so-called "date". I may have had a moderate degree of success with women, but they usually require a little more wooing than one course at an inexpensive restaurant and a short massage around the shoulderblades.'

It was as insulting as it could possibly be, but that was what he wanted. He wanted her to react. And she wouldn't.

'You were the one who invited *me* out—remember?'

'True.'

He removed one hand from where it had been poised over his belt, like some gun-slinger, and rubbed thoughtfully at the darkening shadow which emphasised the masculine jut of his jaw. As macho gestures went, he really couldn't have bettered it, thought Lara weakly.

'But you played the siren, didn't you, Lara? That super-smart confidence at the casting. The way you spoke to me as if you didn't care.' He nodded, as if he had been shown a glimpse into the workings of a criminal mind. 'Very clever. Did someone once tell you that what powerful men crave more than anything is for someone to speak to them as if they aren't? To treat them just like everyone else?'

Lara gave a low laugh. 'I wish I had a tape recorder,' she vowed fervently. 'Then I could play this back to you in the morning—I think that even you might be appalled at your own arrogance and conceit.'

He raised his eyebrows in a mocking challenge. 'It would make for a very interesting morning,' he agreed laconically. 'But, there again, it's going to be an interesting morning anyway—isn't it?'

It took a moment or two for his meaning to sink in, and when it did Lara underwent an uncomfortable sensation of shock coupled with excitement, which made her want to squirm—except she didn't dare to, for fear that he would misinterpret it. Or—even worse—interpret it correctly.

'I hope you aren't suggesting that you're spending the night here? With me!'

'Of course not.'

Lara frowned, feeling like a mouse being teased by a very clever cat. 'You're…not?'

'I'm not suggesting anything, Lara. Just stating a fact. Of course I'll be here in the morning—we're sharing a room.'

It was like that feeling you got when you'd eaten three chocolate biscuits and knew that you were going to eat a fourth, even though you shouldn't.

Lara didn't *want* Darian Wildman anywhere near her. She didn't.

Okay, she did.

But that was on some stupid fundamental level. That was a Lara who didn't exist, wanting to be with a Darian who didn't exist. If only they could be standing here, a man and a woman who had just met…but that was crazy.

If they had only just met then they most definitely *wouldn't* be standing here—and neither would she be wearing just a towel covering her nakedness. A nakedness she was pretty sure he was responding to, judging from that dark, seductive look in his eyes, as if he were running those long, experienced fingers over every single crevice of her body. And yet the contrast between that hot look of desire and the cold contempt which rang from his voice was almost unbearable.

'Darian,' she breathed. 'We…we can't!'

'Can't what?' he enquired unhelpfully.

'We can't share a room together—you know we can't!'

'Afraid that you won't be able to resist me?' he questioned insultingly.

*Yes!* 'No! I will not stay here—not with you!'

'But our host has allotted us this room,' he ground out. 'We cannot question the Sheikh or his judgement.'

'Oh, really?' she demanded furiously. 'He just *happened* to put us in here together, did he? Without any pressure from you?'

'No pressure from me, I can assure you.' He gave a slow smile, pleased to see her give an instinctive little wriggle of frustration, knowing that her body craved him even while her mind fought him. 'He simply asked whether or not we were lovers, and I told him that yes, we were. So here we are,' he finished, on a murmur which somehow managed to sound like a sultry threat.

'We are *not* lovers!' she declared.

'Want to do something about that?' he drawled, and began to unbutton his shirt.

'Darian, stop it!'

'Stop what?'

'Un…' The shirt fluttered to the floor and Lara watched it in fascinated horror, lifting her eyes only to be confronted by the infinitely more disturbing vision of Darian's bare chest—the tawny flesh gleaming enticingly. 'Undressing!' she managed to get out.

'But I have to undress,' he said seriously. 'I'm going to take a shower.'

His belt was unclipped and she heard the rasping of a zip. She closed her eyes in horror.

'I refuse to share a room with you!'

'Then go and tell Khalim that yourself!'

The silky challenge made her open her eyes again, and she wished she hadn't—because he was completely naked. And completely at ease with it.

Lara went hot. Then cold.

'Are you trying to torment me?' she gasped.

He frosted her with an icy smile. 'That's about the most honest thing you've said so far,' he clipped out. 'But then, honesty isn't really your forte, is it, Lara?'

She wanted to appeal to his better judgement. But how could she appeal to anything when now he wasn't just naked, but was showing unmistakable signs of…

She turned her back, biting her teeth down into the flesh

of her bottom lip, hearing his low laugh with something approaching despair as he walked towards the bathroom and slammed the door behind him.

Lara had never dressed more quickly in her life. Whipping through the few outfits she had brought for herself, she slithered into a dress she had bought on a modelling assignment in Singapore. It was a long, fitted dress in bright scarlet silk piped with black—high-necked and skimming her body to fall demurely to her ankles. She controlled the most wayward of her curls with tiny jet-covered clips, applied mascara and lipstick with a trembling hand, and then went over to the bookcase which stood in one corner of the large room, determined to have something to occupy her. Anything to keep her mind and her eyes off the impending and disturbing prospect of Darian emerging from the bathroom…

But it was difficult to concentrate on the book—a beautifully photographed history of Maraban—which would normally have fascinated her. She could hear the splash, splash of the shower, and the sound of Darian singing, loudly and rather tunelessly—as if he hadn't a care in the world.

He seemed to have settled in and coped with his momentous news with amazing ease, she thought, her eyes nearly popping out of her head as she studied a photo of Khalim and Rose's wedding—and her *own* unmistakable profile as she bent to adjust Rose's train!

Darian switched off the powerful jet of water and stepped out of the shower, shaking his dark head slightly as he began to rub the droplets of water away. This felt like a dream from which he would in a minute wake—and he wasn't sure he wanted to.

The emotions he had felt when confronted with what seemed like the uncontradictable truth of his heritage had been varied. There had been confusion, yes—and yet a strange sense of calm, as though the answer to a question he had never dared to ask had finally been given.

Didn't this news of his father's identity make a whole lot about himself clearer and more understandable? That sense of being *different*, of being an outsider, had always burned much stronger in him than in any of the other fatherless boys he had grown up with. It hadn't just been the strange and exotic colour of his skin and the unusual gold of his eyes; it had gone far deeper than that.

Even as a child Darian had always been a loner. He had kept his emotions and his affections severely contained and restrained. So had that been something he'd been born with, or something he had learned along the way?

He had not grown up in an environment where you got close to people, and this was a habit he had carried with him into his adult life. In a way it had made his success more achievable—if you didn't carry around the baggage of close relationships then you had a lot less to distract you from your ambition.

He reflected on the bizarre events of the day, thinking that Khalim, too, had been a surprise—in more than one sense. From making the discovery that he was related to the dark, powerful and enigmatic leader it had proved a disturbingly short step to discovering that he might actually like him—maybe even form some kind of tenuous bond with him.

He didn't know what the outcome of this strange and totally unexpected visit to Maraban would be, and for once in his life it didn't bother him. Usually Darian liked everything mapped out, to know where he was going and what he was doing, but suddenly he recognised that sometimes you just had to go with the flow.

In fact, the only shadow on the current landscape took

the form of the woman he could hear moving around in the adjoining room. His mouth twisted with a mixture of contempt and desire.

What could have been a straightforward—if highly unusual—state of affairs had been complicated and made distasteful by the behaviour of Lara Black.

He felt the slow, steady pulsing of his heart, wondering why it should bother him—why he couldn't just dismiss the thought of her. Heaven knew, he usually managed that just fine. But she was like an itch. Something niggling away at him, stinging at his skin and making him feel aware of her in a way he didn't want to be. He needed to get her completely out of his system, he decided grimly, and there was one surefire way to do that.

But this time Lara would fight him all the way, he recognised, and somehow that sharpened his senses even more. He gave a slow smile of anticipation as he wrapped a towel around his narrow hips and sauntered back into the bedroom.

She was lost in the book she had been reading, but at the sound of his footfall she automatically looked up and her mouth dried. 'Oh, I see you've bothered to put something on,' she observed caustically, even though her heart was thudding away like a piston.

His fingers hovered provocatively over the knot of the towel at his hip and he raised his eyebrows mockingly. 'Is that disapproval I hear in your voice, Lara? You'd prefer me to lose it, would you?'

She swallowed down the infuriating desire to say yes. 'I'll just carry on reading my book while you get dressed,' she said, then glanced at her watch. 'Better hurry up,' she added sweetly. 'Khalim is not a man who should be kept waiting.'

She saw him shrug and then stared unseeingly at the words on the page, listening while he pulled on his clothes, not saying a word. The silence seemed to grow until it became huge and unwelcome. And suddenly all Lara's doubts and fears and uncertainties began to nag at her. She was angry at him for all kinds of complex reasons, but deep down she feared that her main motive was self-seeking. Wasn't she angry because he had shown a decided lack of interest in her as a person—because she had started to fall for him in a big way and he clearly hadn't reciprocated her feelings? And wasn't that a rather shameful reason for helping to maintain this sizzling undercurrent of tension between them? What good was that going to do any of them?

Maybe it was up to her to try and make peace.

She waited until he had slipped his shoes on, and then looked up to see him running his fingers through still-damp hair.

'Darian?' she said quietly.

The look he gave her was deliberately impartial—but then he wasn't foolish enough to get himself worked up into a state of sexual desire just before dinner, not when there wasn't enough time to see it through to its ultimate conclusion. 'Yes, Lara?'

She closed the pages of the book and put her fingertips on the soft leather which bound it. 'I'm sorry that I deceived you.'

'Sorry that you deceived me?' he questioned tonelessly. 'Or just sorry that I found out?'

'But it was inevitable that you would find out!' she argued. 'You must understand why I wanted to get to know you before I decided what action to take about the letter—why, you could have been any kind of maniac, for all I knew!'

'As opposed to a red-hot stud, you mean?'

'You flatter yourself, Darian.'

Their eyes met, his gaze boring into her until her cheeks

began to burn. 'Oh, I don't think so,' he said softly. 'You may be an actress, Lara, and a very good one at that—but I know enough about women to realise that you weren't faking it.'

She slapped her palms to her hot cheeks. 'Don't!'

'Don't speak the truth? No, I can see that might bother someone with your morals.'

This was just getting worse instead of better. She drew a deep breath, hoping to appeal to his sense of reason—to something…anything that would make him stop looking at her with that reluctant desire which made her feel so small.

'Surely you can understand why I didn't mention anything to you, Darian? At least not until I'd spoken to Khalim? I've known him and Rose for a long time—I didn't know you at all!'

'But you sure knew me better after dinner, didn't you?' He gave a low and insulting laugh. 'Did you want to make sure that the brother to the Sheikh fulfilled *all* the criteria for being a man?'

Her temper snapped. 'Now you are wilfully twisting everything I say! I had no intention of letting you make love to me that night. It just…it just…happened,' she finished lamely.

'Does it happen a lot for you that way?' he enquired, with the sardonic air of someone asking an unnecessary question.

'Never!' she retorted. 'I told you that at the time!'

'So it *was* just me,' he mused. 'In which case—I *should* be flattered.' He lowered his voice to a sultry promise. 'It was pretty good for me, too, Lara, if you really want to know—which makes me wonder why you're being so unnecessarily prim. After all, if you had sex with me when we barely knew each other, then I should have thought you would be eager to repeat the experience now that we're so much better acquainted.' He smiled as he let his gaze travel to the huge brocade-covered bed. 'It seems a bit of a waste of a good opportunity otherwise, don't you think?'

He couldn't have made it sound more mechanical if he had tried—a man and a woman who were fiercely attracted to one another—simply making use of the facilities on offer! But while Darian might have a heart of stone Lara was simply not made that way.

She opened her mouth to tell him that he was the last person on the planet she would ever get intimate with after what he had said to her, but at that precise moment there was a light rap on the door.

Darian raised his eyebrows. 'Shall we continue this fascinating conversation later?' he drawled. 'I think we're being summoned to dinner.'

## CHAPTER ELEVEN

THE table was set in a small banqueting room—a surprisingly intimate table, even though it was laid with plates of solid gold which gleamed beneath the light from the dazzling chandelier overhead. Heavy crystal glasses threw off rainbow lights, and overblown crimson roses were crammed into low golden bowls.

'Isn't it beautiful?' Lara breathed automatically.

Darian turned to look at her, at the elegant little curve of her nose and the way her soft lips had parted. She had clipped some of her hair back—he had never seen it like that before. The rampant curls had been subdued, emphasising her long, elegant neck, and the overall impression was to make her look rather pure and innocent. But then, she was an actress, he reminded himself. A chameleon. She wore so many different masks.

'Exquisite,' he said curtly, his head turning as Khalim walked into the room accompanied by a retinue of servants, most of whom he dismissed immediately.

He had changed from his Western suit into one of the garments tradionally worn by the Marabanesh—only his was fashioned from the finest silk, denoting his royal status. It was a fluid and flowing robe in a silvery colour which made Lara think of a river. He indicated for them to take their seats and ran a finger reflectively over a rose in one of the bowls, rather in the way that Lara had done in her room, earlier.

'You know, it is a strict rule at the palace to have only roses placed on the table at royal functions,' he said gravely as he took his seat, though his black eyes were glinting with mischief. 'In honour of my darling Rose.'

Lara frowned as she unfolded the heavy linen napkin. 'Won't Rose think it strange you haven't told her I'm here, Khalim? Won't she be upset?'

'Why would she be?' Khalim looked at her steadily. 'Rose loves me and trusts me,' he said simply. 'And she trusts my judgement,' he added softly. 'She will know soon enough, when the time is right, but she must not be troubled by events over which she has no control. Especially not now, when she carries my child within her.'

He spoke in a way in which few men did—his words were poetic and romantic and they came straight from the heart. Lara had not spent her life looking for love—women who did that were doomed, in her opinion—but as she listened she experienced a great ache of longing. She tried to imagine what it must be like to have a man profess his love for you in such a profound and moving way as that. Didn't Rose have what most women dreamed of? Oh, not the prince or the palaces or the untold riches—but the steadfast and passionate love of the man she adored.

And what a man Khalim was. She recognised then that somewhere in the back of her mind she had thought that no man could ever match someone like Khalim—his strength and his passion and his sheer, overriding masculinity. Only now she had met another such man.

Covertly, she studied Darian from beneath her lashes. His half-brother had those same qualities—qualities which had been born in him, not fashioned by his upbringing in a place of riches and privilege. Darian would be a man whose love would be worth more than a king's ransom.

And she had blown it.

'You will drink some wine, Darian?' Khalim was saying.

'No, thanks.' Darian pointed to a decanter filled with a rich gold liquid. 'I'll have some of what you're having.'

Khalim nodded, looking pleased. 'It is a special Maraban concoction—made from honey and water taken from the crystal streams of mountain rivers and scented with rose and cinnamon.'

Darian took the goblet and sipped some. 'Here,' he murmured, and passed the goblet to Lara.

The gesture seemed somehow symbolic of sharing, and yet at the same time a mockery. Part of her wanted to refuse—but how could she in front of Khalim, and risk appearing churlish or rude? The goblet was so heavy and her fingers were so unsteady that she had to hold onto it with two hands. 'Th—thanks,' she stumbled.

The glittering look he sent her was impenetrable, and Lara found herself wondering how she was going to be able to fight him off later, when they were alone in their sumptuous room. Especially when there was a part of her which didn't want to fight him at all…

A feast was brought before them—dish after tiny dish of subtly flavoured delicacies, some of which Lara had tasted before and some of which were new to her. She looked at the mound of glistening saffron-scented rice, studded with pistachios and cardamom seeds, and tried to summon up an appetite for it.

But during the meal she found herself cast in the role of spectator, listening while Darian continued to ask questions about Maraban's history and about Khalim's ongoing task of making sure that the country embraced new technology while losing nothing of its tradition and traditional values. She could have listened all night to the Prince describing dark conquests, the battles of his ancestors as they strove to liberate Maraban from marauding neighbouring countries.

'Tomorrow we shall ride,' announced Khalim as tiny little cups of thick, dark coffee were placed before them.

Darian dropped a single sugar cube into his cup and absently stirred at it. 'I've never ridden before.'

'It alarms you?'

Darian's eyes narrowed into golden shards. 'On the contrary. I have always enjoyed rising to a challenge.'

'Of course. But I shall give you our quietest mount.'

'Oh, no, you won't.' Darian's voice was low, but it carried with it a steely determination, and Lara couldn't miss the unmistakable look of horror which crossed the face of one of the servants. You wouldn't need to speak English to be aware that this guest was arguing with the Prince!

'I will take a mount that you favour,' Darian emphasised.

This time Khalim frowned. 'But it would be sheer folly to put a novice on a spirited horse!'

'And would you not do the same in my situation?' challenged Darian softly.

The eyes of the two men clashed a silent duel over the ornate table, until at last Khalim nodded his head.

'Indeed I would.'

There was silence for a moment, as if another unspoken test had been set and passed.

'And can I come and watch?' asked Lara.

They turned to look at her, as if they had forgotten she was there.

'Of course you can,' said Khalim indulgently. 'You don't mind, Darian?'

'Why should I mind?' But of course Darian did mind. He minded a lot. He had never ridden before, and as Khalim had pointed out he *was* a novice. Did he really want Lara to witness him at the very bottom of a learning curve—he who liked to be seen to be accomplished in all things?

'Good. That is settled.' Khalim rose to his feet. 'You will forgive me if I leave you now? I have affairs of state to attend to, and I must telephone Rose before she retires. You may linger here, over coffee—or one of the servants will show you where a television can be found, should you wish it. Or…' His voice softened. 'You can take Lara for a walk through the rose gardens—they are smaller than those at the Golden Palace, but they are beautiful indeed, and the perfect place for lovers on such a starlit evening.'

Lara opened her mouth to protest, to end this ridiculous charade here and now, but before she could speak Darian had answered for her.

'Thanks, but I think we'll go straight to bed. Lara's very tired—aren't you, darling?'

The mock concern in his voice made her want to rail against him. But what could she possibly say that would not embarrass her host? She nodded, and even managed to curve her lips into a smile. 'Very tired,' she agreed demurely.

She saw Khalim narrow his eyes fractionally. 'Then I will bid you both goodnight and sweet dreams.'

They listened to the sound of his retreating footsteps as they echoed down the marble corridor, and then Darian bent his head to speak softly in her ear.

'Why, Lara—you smiled like you almost meant it then,' he murmured. 'How useful it must be to have a talent for acting—you can use it in any given situation!'

The subtle masculine scent of him was playing havoc with her senses. She wanted to sway against him, to have him hold her close to him, to kiss her and blot out all this pain and uncertainty. But she fought it, turning on him instead. 'How dare you imply that we can't wait to get back to our room for a night of hot, no-holds-barred sex?'

Well, it was pretty easy to read what was uppermost in *her* mind. 'Is that what I was doing?' he questioned innocently, but the ache in his body felt far from innocent. 'Then we'd better make our way back, hadn't we—and quickly? I should hate to keep you waiting for your hot, no-holds-barred sex, Lara!'

Her eyes flashed blue fury at him, but she kept a tight rein on it. She would hang onto her dignity. She wasn't going to answer him back there and then. Not with a silent servant guiding them back to their quarters. Still, he was labouring under a very big misapprehension indeed if he thought that she was about to leap into bed with him.

The servant opened their door and Lara went straight into the bathroom without a word. She locked the door behind her, not emerging until her face was scrubbed clean and her teeth brushed. She was wearing a pair of pyjamas which, though light and silky for the sultry temperature, could by no stretch of the imagination ever be described as sexy.

Darian looked up from where he had been flicking through the book she had been reading earlier. He had removed his cuff-links, she noted, but that was all.

'Finished in the bathroom, *darling*?' he questioned sardonically.

'It's all yours.' Lara hesitated, then pointedly looked at the long, low divan which stood underneath the shuttered windows. 'That divan looks very comfortable, doesn't it?'

'Indeed it does,' he agreed gravely. 'I imagine it's probably just as comfortable as the bed. One would be certain to get a good night's sleep on it, anyway.'

'Absolutely,' said Lara, relieved, and yet annoyingly just a bit infuriated, too. She hadn't expected him to agree quite so gracefully! And didn't you want him to try and make you put up a bit of a fight? taunted a rogue voice inside her head. Weren't you looking forward to at least one impassioned kiss before you finally pushed him away?

Darian saw her face and gave a small smile as he walked

towards the bathroom. For someone who made her living from acting she could be remarkably transparent at times!

He undressed and showered, glad of the heavy beat of the cool water to subdue unwanted appetites and bring him back to some degree of normality. For it would be all too easy to get carried away—to be seduced by life out here in this strange, magical land, where men really did seem to live as they were born to.

He thought of the traffic crushes and the noise and pollution of the city, and his mouth twisted as he turned off the shower jets. Did places like this always inject you with a kind of wistfulness? he wondered. He couldn't even blame the wine at dinner, since he hadn't had any! He shook his head slightly, dispersing droplets of water and reflecting that he was badly in need of a reality check.

When he returned to the bedroom Lara was lying in bed, the covers right up to her neck, her eyes tightly closed.

'Asleep already?' he mocked softly.

She didn't reply, taking care to make her breathing as slow and as steady and as deep as if she really *was* asleep.

It was torture, just lying there, hearing the unhurried removal of his clothes. She wanted to tell him to turn the wretched light off, but if she did that then he would know she wasn't asleep, and would probably start to engage her in conversation.

Or worse…

She wanted to squirm, too. Her pyjamas felt hot and constricting, burning against her skin where the material touched. And her pulse was hammering so loudly that she was amazed he hadn't heard it and made some hateful remark about it. Her breasts were all tingling and tight, and…

He heard the almost inaudible change in the pace of her breathing. Now it sounded shallow, and rapid. Darian smiled as he snapped the light off and climbed into bed.

As the bed dipped beneath his weight Lara sat up as if she'd been electrocuted—and with the nearness and warmth of his naked body she might as well have been. 'What the hell do you think you're doing?'

He yawned. 'Going to sleep. Why—did you have something else in mind?'

She snapped the light on with shaking fingers, still shocked and yet excited beyond belief to see him arrogantly sprawled out next to her, not even having bothered to cover up the bare tawny chest.

'You're not sleeping here!'

'Yes, I am.'

'But...but you said...you said you'd sleep on the divan!' she spluttered.

Darian shook his head. 'No, I didn't, Lara. You commented on how comfortable it looked. I agreed, and you mistakenly took that to mean that I would be sleeping on it. Well, you were wrong. This bed is big enough for both of us, and I am not, repeat *not* sleeping on the divan!'

'You don't think that as a *gentleman*, you might offer to take it?'

'But I never claimed to be a gentleman.' The golden eyes glittered. 'Just as you never claimed to be a lady.'

'I'm not going to react to that.'

'Suits me.'

Now he was punching the pillow around with his fist, rearranging it, and Lara stared at him in disbelief. 'And that's your last word on the subject?'

'I think we've said just about everything there is to say on the subject of beds and divans, don't you?' he questioned, his voice bored.

'Well, if you won't sleep there—I will!'

'Fine.'

He turned over and shut his eyes, and Lara stared at him

with mounting frustration and indignation. He meant it! He actually meant it!

Well, so did she! She grabbed her pillow and one of the covers, hastily turning her head rather than be confronted by the sight of the remaining covers clinging so lovingly to his long, lean frame.

And she had been wrong—the divan was not comfortable at all. It had probably been designed for a woman to lie on alluringly, showing off her body for her sheikh, not for a tall, tired woman to try and get eight hours' sleep on.

Lara tossed and turned, her frustration mounting as she heard Darian's immediate steady breathing. As the night wore on tiredness gave way to anger and hot tears began to scald at the corners of her eyes. She felt alone and afraid and abandoned.

That's only because it's the middle of the night, she told herself. The lowest ebb of all is the hour just before dawn, when you seem to be the only person in the world.

Darian woke to a sound. A little sniff. In the darkness, he frowned, wanting to ignore it, but there it was again, another tiny little sound, and he sighed. 'Why are you crying, Lara?' he asked softly.

'I'm not.'

'I know this must be a difficult concept for you to embrace, but couldn't you just try telling the truth for once?' he drawled sardonically.

She contemplated ignoring him, but just the sound of his voice reached out and comforted her, like a warm fire. A human voice in the dead of night. 'Why do you think? It's bloody uncomfortable on this thing!'

'Well, you do have a choice,' he remarked sagely.

Yes, she did. She could lie here like a martyr, or she could take a little decisive action. Picking up her pillow, she walked back over to the vast bed and slid in beside him, taking care to lie on the very edge.

'Be careful you don't slip off.'

His voice sounded amused, and it was the amusement which finally made the anger and frustration inside her snap. She flicked the light on, sat up and glared at him, spirals of hair tumbling all over her face. She impatiently pushed them away with the back of her hand.

'Just why did you bring me here, Darian?'

'It seemed like a good idea at the time.'

'I'm serious!' she hissed.

He could see that. The woman who had so entranced him with her feistiness at the casting was back. And how. Her cheeks flamed like roses and her eyes sparked a bright sapphire fire. His eyes drifted to her breasts and he felt his body jerk in reaction.

'Why do you think I asked you?' he asked tightly. 'Because I was angry with you.'

'Surely if you were angry with me then the most sensible solution would have been to wish me as far away as possible?'

'But sense doesn't come into it when sex is involved,' he said bluntly. 'Does it?'

His voice was curt, almost cruel. 'No,' she said flatly. 'It doesn't.'

He had planned to have his fill of her. To make love to her over and over again, in every way and in every position. To learn every inch of her body like a man conquering a brand-new country. And only when he had done that would he move on and forget her.

But the time had not been right. Not before dinner, and strangely enough not now, even though they were in bed together and he was naked beside her.

If it had been any other woman he would have started to kiss her. He was experienced enough to kiss away her doubts and have her sighing with pleasure, a consummate enough lover to know how to make her beg for him. But he saw the dried track of a tear, the sudden tremble of her mouth, and something stopped him and he knew that he could not. Not when she looked so cold and so lost and so damned vulnerable.

She's just *acting* again, he told himself furiously, but that didn't seem to make any difference. And deep down he didn't think she was acting at all—she wouldn't bother pretending not to have been crying quietly in the dark if she was, would she? He got out of bed and slid on a pair of boxer shorts before climbing back in.

'What are you doing now?' she asked, a slight tinge of hysteria to her voice.

'Allaying your fears that I might try it on in the middle of the night,' he said gravely. 'See? I'm quite decent now, Lara.'

Decent? If he had swathed himself from head to toe in voluminous sackcloth, then 'decent' would still be the last word she would have used. And now she was confused—from being fearful that he *would* try it on, that she would have trouble resisting him, her self-esteem had taken a great plummet. Didn't he want her any more?

'Come here,' he said, almost gently, and pulled her against him.

'No.' She tried to resist the impact of that warm, living flesh. 'Go away,' she mumbled, but she didn't move.

He smoothed the silken tumble of her curls, thinking how soft they felt, the scent of her shampoo drifting towards his nostrils with its wholesome fragrance. For the first time in his life he felt disarmed by a sense of protectiveness—he didn't know how and he didn't know why. He just knew that it couldn't have come at a more unwelcome time. 'Just go to sleep, Lara,' he sighed.

With one final sniff she snuggled against him, and it felt

like coming home. Like walking into a room with a fire when you had been outside in the cold. But that was all an illusion, she reminded herself. A wish and a dream and a desire—all mixed up in her head and a million miles away from reality simply because she *was* a million miles from reality.

Yet the warmth of his embrace was irresistible, as was the rhythmic movement of his hand stroking her hair as he lulled her into a state of utter defencelessness. She couldn't have moved if she'd wanted to, and she didn't want to.

Her last thought before drifting off into a fitful and dreamless sleep was that this was the kind of thing you should do with a man before you had sex with him. Being intimate without being too intimate. Building something slowly instead of grabbing at it. She felt like a child who had gobbled all the icing off the top of the cake. And how she wished she hadn't.

When Lara's eyelids fluttered open, it was to find Darian's space beside her empty. In fact, the room was empty. She blinked her eyes and rubbed them just as the door opened and in he walked, carrying a pile of clothes. Her heart flipped over when she saw him.

It's just because he's wearing jodhpurs, she thought—all men looked good in jodhpurs.

The cream trousers defined every sinew of his muscular thighs, clinging to the narrow jut of his hips and the high, hard curve of his buttocks. His shirt was loose and cool, though the fine, filmy material did nothing to disguise the rocky torso and the broad span of his shoulders. Long, soft black leather riding boots completed the ensemble, and for the first time in her life Lara understood why leather was considered synonymous with sex.

But sex was not what she wanted from Darian, she realised, her heart sinking. Or rather, not sex on its own. She wanted more. She wanted affection and respect and tenderness and regard. There was a word for what she desired, and that word was love.

And, judging by the cool, non-committal look on his face, she wanted far more than she could ever have.

'Good morning,' she said, feeling almost more shy than if they *had* had sex.

'You slept.' It was a statement. He knew it for fact simply because he had not. The moment she had got into bed with him had been the moment when sleep became, for him, a distant memory.

He must have been out of his head. Playing the protector and the carer when all he'd really wanted to do was drive himself into her sweet and yielding flesh, over and over again. Punishing his body with the nearness of hers and the sweet, feminine scent of her which had invaded his senses until the sun had risen, and unable to do a damned thing about it. He had never known such an acute and excruciating sense of frustration in his life.

'Yes. Yes, I did get to sleep,' she agreed. 'Eventually.' This was awful—she felt as if he was someone she had just met in the doctor's waiting room. She looked instead at the pile of clothes he was carrying. 'What's that?'

He dropped it onto the foot of the bed. 'Riding clothes,' he said shortly. 'Khalim sent them for you. They belong to Rose and he says you're pretty much the same size. I've eaten breakfast and I'm just off to the stables—so do join us when you're ready. If you're still inclined to.'

The dark, unfriendly note in his voice told her that he would rather she didn't, and with something which she supposed was a smile he was gone, leaving Lara staring after him, wondering what she had done to make him look as if he had been eating something with a distinctly sour taste. Was it sexual frustration he felt? Or frustration that he *had* actually ended up playing the gentleman?

Wasn't it crazy that just lying innocently in his arms, with him stroking her hair like that, should have made her feel so…so…dreamy? But tenderness could mean so much more than even the most spectacular orgasm in the world. Even if it *was* only pretend tenderness.

She showered and put the riding clothes on. Khalim was right—the two women were pretty similar in size, though Lara was taller and, judging by the shirt, her breasts were now smaller than Rose's. But Rose had had one child already, and everyone knew that pregnancy changed your shape.

Lara stared in the mirror, at her slim hips and breasts untouched by childbirth, and a sudden yearning stabbed at her. Babies were something she had never even considered before, yet now she saw a sharp, snapshot image of a baby at her breast, a beautiful baby with golden eyes and dark ruffled hair.

Stop it, she thought impatiently. Just stop it. He's gorgeous and he's a challenge. He's good in bed, and occasionally he can be tender—but that's all. You aren't in love with him, and he certainly isn't in love with *you*.

And she tied her hair back so tightly that it made her wince, then set off for the stables.

# CHAPTER TWELVE

LARA burst into a peal of laughter and was met with a furious gold stare.

'It isn't funny,' he growled.

'Oh, I'm sorry, Darian, but it is. Very.' She held her hand out to him. 'Here.'

He eyed it suspiciously for a moment before grasping it, and then swung himself up from the dust onto which he had just tumbled, bringing himself right up close to Lara, enjoying the immediate darkening of her eyes.

'Do you like watching me fall, Lara?'

Actually, it was strange watching him not being perfectly proficient at something, to see him cast in the role of novice. Strange and almost *endearing*. If it had been anyone else she might have said *cute*, except that four-letter words like *nice* and *cute* didn't really sit well on Darian.

'A fallen man?' she mused. 'Yes, I *do* think I like it!' She could smell the sweat on him, and it gleamed on his skin as brilliantly as on the highly polished flanks of the Akhal-Teke horse from which he had just plummeted.

He let go of her hand and placed both his own on the horse again.

'You're getting back up?' she asked, in surprise.

'Isn't that the first rule of riding?' he questioned. 'That you get straight back on?'

She nodded as he swung himself up. He was persistent; she would say that for him. From having been shown the rudiments of riding by Khalim himself, he had persevered with learning the new skill every spare minute, like a man driven to conquer.

He was up by first light, out helping the grooms to muck the horses out. He told her that he was determined to learn as much as possible about this creature who seemed so reluctant to have him on its back. Lara was quickly learning that there were no half-measures where Darian Wildman was concerned.

Khalim had found him the most beautiful palomino—the usual metallic sheen even more pronounced in this case. The horse's coat gleamed as golden as the eyes of the man who rode him. And when he did manage to stay astride Darian made the most magnificent vision, Lara was forced to admit. Though that shouldn't have surprised her. Nothing really surprised her where he was concerned.

The night when he had held her in his arms had completed her captivation. He had disarmed her with his gentleness, leaving her happily open to the suggestion that they become lovers once more. Except that no such suggestion had been made, and neither had that comforting and innocent night been repeated—because Darian had taken to sleeping on the uncomfortable divan beneath the window.

*She* was the one all alone in the big, comfortable bed now, and *she* was the one who was lying awake until the small hours, while he slept as deeply as a child.

'How's that?' he called.

She watched him trot around the dusty paddock and nodded. 'Better,' she called back. 'But not so tight on the reins!'

He relaxed his grip by a fraction, enjoying the feel of the powerful animal between his thighs. He was getting the hang of this riding thing now, and about time, too. It had been galling to accept that not only was Khalim a superb rider but that Lara was, too. All those years of wholesome upbringing in the English countryside had made her into a confident horsewoman. She looked good on a horse—but then she looked good doing just about anything.

They had been here for just over a week, and this morning Khalim had had to go off to meet with a visiting dignitary and had left Lara in charge of Darian's riding lessons.

'You will take my place and teach him?' he'd asked her softly.

Lara enjoyed the flash of irritation which sparked from the golden eyes. 'Of course. I'll enjoy cracking the whip!' she joked.

'You can try,' Darian whispered softly.

Lara looked down at the dusty ground, afraid that Khalim would see the naked look of desire in her eyes, and afraid that Darian would see it, too. Horseriding was supposed to be an innocent pursuit, yet somehow he had managed to make the atmosphere heavy with tension and expectation—shimmering like the heat from the sun above them.

'You won't mind taking orders from a woman?' she questioned, once Khalim had gone.

His tone was dry. 'It will be another new experience.'

'And do you enjoy new experiences?' she asked, her eyes slanting at him.

Darian smiled. 'Oh, yes,' he murmured.

She was flirting with him again, he noted now. Indeed, she had been doing that ever since the night when he had held her so chastely in his arms. Women could be so contrary. Put something out of reach and they immediately wanted it! But the trouble was that now the boot was on the other foot he wasn't sure that *he* wanted it. Not any more.

Because sex with Lara would be complicated this time

around. He recognised that with a grim kind of certainty. And wasn't his life complicated enough already? So much had happened—and not just between the two of them. He was only just getting used to the fact that he had a brother, a brother who he was getting to know little by little—not easy when both were men who rarely let their guard down, Darian through instinct and Khalim through necessity.

The two of them would sit up late at night, talking—sometimes into the early hours. They had described their childhoods to each other, and Darian had done his best not to feel envy at the privilege of Khalim's early years. But the Prince had sensed it with an intuitive sensitivity.

'Yes, I had the riches, Darian,' he had said softly. 'But you were given the gift of freedom. Riches can be earned, but complete freedom cannot—not when you carry the responsibilities which come with having royal blood.'

It was a different way of looking at things—but then, didn't this place make you look at things differently anyway? And, yes, Khalim had all the burdens and responsibilities which came with governing his country—but his life was clearly defined in ways that Darian was growing to envy.

Because for all the paraphernalia and trappings which came with his royal status—the palaces and the servants—Khalim enjoyed such simple pleasures. Perhaps it was because his riches had always been taken for granted that he was able to look beyond material things. It was another lesson to be learnt.

Khalim had taken Darian walking beneath the star-filled skies, pointing out constellations which were not visible even from his penthouse apartment in London. There were no cars out here in the isolated splendour of the countryside which surrounded the palace. Nor noise, nor crowds.

In fact, the only blot on this surreal landscape remained Lara herself. With his self-imposed sexual limits, he had begun to get to know her. And to like her. Even though liking her was something he had tried to put up barriers against, telling himself that she was an actress, that she had deceived him, and if she could do it once she could do it again.

Which was why he had taken up riding with such fervour. Apart from wanting to excel at it—which was inherent in his nature—he also used it as a form of diversion, driving himself at it, hour after hour, so that by the time he fell onto that damned concrete block of a divan he was so bushed that he slept the night through.

And he would be lying if he did not admit to taking a certain amount of pleasure at the sight of Lara's dark-rimmed eyes which met his each morning.

A servant arrived, bearing a tray of iced orange water, and he watched while he set it down in the shade and Lara sat down prettily in her jodhpurs and beckoned him over.

His throat felt dry as he dismounted, but it was a dryness caused by more than mere thirst. Khalim had gone, and for the first time it was just the two of them. As he approached he could see the shape of her breasts peaking beneath the fine silk shirt, and he felt the debilitating jerk of desire as he imagined slowly peeling the shirt from her body.

Forget it, he told himself. Lara's trouble. She's been trouble since the moment you first set eyes on her, and if you get involved with her then there's plenty more where that came from.

But that didn't stop him from issuing a curt command to the groom, who bowed his head in response.

Lara had been watching the little interchange and looked up at him in surprise as he approached. 'Wasn't that Marabanese you were speaking to the groom?'

'It was.'

'Who taught you?'

The golden eyes glittered. 'Khalim has been instructing me in the basics of the language.'

He sat down beside her, took the glass from her and drank deeply, putting the empty glass down and wiping his lips with the back of his hand.

'You're acting more and more like a sheikh every day!' she teased.

'Yeah.' He stared moodily into the middle distance.

'And sounding like one, too!' She wished she knew what was going on in that head of his. She'd thought they were supposed to have abandoned hostilities and declared an unspoken truce of sorts. Were they or were they not able to exist in relative harmony? In theory, yes, of course they were—except that there was this terrible hunger bubbling away inside her. An overwhelming longing to feel his lips on hers once more.

Maybe it was one-sided. Maybe he just didn't feel it any more and the way she had deceived him had killed his desire for her stone-dead. They were sharing a bedroom, but that was the one place she barely saw him. He crept into the bedroom in the early hours, completely ignoring her and the large, empty space in the bed beside her, and was gone when she woke in the morning.

She watched while the groom led the horse away. 'Exotically beautiful, isn't he?' she remarked.

'Mmm,' he said, non-committally.

'They're a unique breed, you know.'

'Are they?'

Lara drew a breath. 'Yep. Arguably the oldest surviving cultured equine breed.'

'You don't say?'

Well, she had to say *something*, or else she was going to come out with something like, *Don't you find me attractive any more, Darian?*

'They're known for their speed, stamina and intelligence,' she continued, the words coming out in a flurry.

He turned his head to look at her, drowning in the blue of her eyes, then looked away again. 'A little like me, then?'

Her heart pounded. 'A little, I guess.'

There was a split-second pause, and when he spoke his voice was lazy. 'What else about them, Lara?'

'They're hot-bloods, definitely not warm-bloods.'

He didn't say anything.

'And unusually sensitive to the way they are treated,' she rushed on. 'They're responsive to gentle training, and can be stubborn or resentful if treated rudely.' She paused and held her breath as he turned to her again, only this time he didn't look away. 'A little like me, in fact.'

He saw the pulse at her temple begin a frantic little beat, and suddenly all his defences left him. He brushed a line over the fine skin there and felt its throbbing beneath his fingertip. 'Is that so?' he murmured.

'Y-yes.' She held her breath as his fingertip traced its way down her cheek, lingering on the line of her jaw, then down to the hollow of her neck. She could feel the flutter of her heart and the honey-rush of sweet desire, but she didn't dare move. It was like being in the middle of a spell—one wrong word or gesture and it would be broken, and she would be back to frustrated longing once again.

'What else?' he murmured, only now his fingertip was teasing the tip of her breast.

Lara swallowed. 'Their eyes are…'

'Are what, Lara?' He felt the nipple bud and harden and he sucked in a breath.

'Are l-large and expressive. And sometimes almond-shaped.'

The golden blaze almost blinded her. 'Like your eyes,' he observed softly. 'What else?'

Now his hand was drifting down over her torso and she could scarcely breathe.

'Tell me, Lara,' he urged. 'I want to know.'

'Their…their bodies are long and lean.' She swallowed again. 'The muscling well-defined, s-smoothly hugging the bone.'

'That's me,' he whispered. 'Isn't it?'

By now his fingertip had edged down to the fork in her legs, drifting forward and back, forward and back, so that Lara closed her eyes and gasped.

'Isn't it, Lara?'

'Well, yes. You know it is.'

'Don't you want to feel for yourself how it feels?' he purred. 'Feel the muscle which hugs the bone…?'

She didn't need to be asked twice. Her hands flew to his chest, feeling the masculine heat of him through the damp shirt, and all the while his finger continued its erotic little dance, the material of the jodhpurs both restricting and heightening her pleasure.

'Darian!' she gasped.

'Mmm?'

'We can't do this here!'

'Do what?' he questioned innocently, enjoying the way her thighs were now parting, revelling in the urgent little grind of her hips. 'We're not doing anything, are we? Not really. I'm just playing with you a little. Touching you there.' He felt her squirm. 'And *there*.' He increased the pressure of his finger and her head fell back.

'Someone might come!' she protested, in a thick, slurred voice which didn't sound like her own.

'I think someone might,' he agreed unsteadily. 'But all the grooms have gone, if that's what you're worried about.'

Too late, she realised just where he was taking her. 'Kiss me, Darian,' she pleaded on a moan. 'Please. Just kiss me.'

'No.'

The single word should have terminated her pleasure with all the finality of a bucket of cold water being thrown over her, but it did no such thing. If anything, the cold, harsh word only increased her ascent into that tantalising, nebulous place which made such mockery of almost everything else which existed. Maybe she wasn't so like the Akhal-Teke at all, she thought desperately, for there was no resentment on her part about the way he was treating her—and shouldn't there have been? *Shouldn't there have been?*

But then it happened, great wave upon wave of engulfing pleasure, and she opened her mouth, the pleasure so intense that she wanted to scream. And that was when he kissed her at last, swallowing up her cries with the fierce, hard pressure of his mouth, clamping his hand possessively over her jodhpurs while she still pulsed with sweet, dying spasms and her head fell uselessly to his shoulder.

'Oh,' she moaned. It was a helpless little cry, and it was edged with sorrow as well as fulfillment—for hadn't the kiss been merely a silencing technique instead of a demonstration of affection?

'Touch me,' he urged. 'Please.'

Her hand moved down and her eyes snapped open. 'Oh!' she breathed. He was hard, so very, very hard.

'Yes—oh,' he murmured wryly.

'Wh-what do you want to do now?'

'I want you,' he shuddered. 'That's what I want. And I want you to undress me. Now.'

She felt the flush move from her neck to her cheeks, so that they burned like fire. It was a stark and unequivocal sexual command, dark with promise but devoid of all tenderness. 'Wouldn't you rather go back to our room?'

He was sliding her jodhpurs down now, with difficulty.

'Practically?' He groaned. 'Lara, I don't think I can. Take your boots off.'

With trembling hands she obeyed him, sliding the soft leather down over her calves and kicking them off into the dust.

'Now, come here,' he said softly. 'Come here, Lara.' And he lifted her up, slithering her jodhpurs and her panties away with one brief, economical movement, then lowering her down on top of him, closing his eyes and groaning again as he felt himself encased in her tight, molten heat. 'Oh, yes,' he bit out. 'Oh, yes!'

She held onto his shoulders and began to move.

He opened his eyes and watched her through his lashes. 'Ride me, Lara,' he urged thickly. 'Ride me.'

She abandoned all restraint and misgivings, and all inhibitions, too, forgetting everything except just how delicious it felt, with the hot sun beating down on her and the hot feel of him inside her. She closed her eyes and let her hips slide towards him so that he filled her completely, and she gave a soft, low moan of pleasure as they began to move in rhythm.

Darian was lost in a place more magical than Maraban, his hands holding onto her slender hips as she moved on him and around him, feeling the warmth rise and rise until he heard her shattered and disbelieving little cries once more. And then it was impossible to contain his own pleasure for a second longer as his world split into a thousand shards of sharp-edged ecstasy.

There was silence, bar the distant sound of the mountain wind the Marabanesh called the *rabi*, which seemed to echo the sounds of their small, gasping breaths.

Lara wiped the palm of her hand over her damp, flushed cheeks and looked down at him, just as the thick black lashes parted and the golden eyes gleamed up at her.

She wanted to bend her head to kiss him, but this did

not seem to be the kind of situation which demanded soft and tender kisses. What had just happened had been fulfilling, yes, but in a purely physical way, she recognised with a heavy heart. She wanted more than just physical perfection—but he was not the man to give her more than that.

'I'd better move—' she began, but he halted her with a touch to her belly, making her shiver.

'No, don't. Not yet. Stay there—just for a minute.'

'But the grooms—'

'They won't return. I told them not to.'

Lara raised her eyebrows in surprise. 'I didn't know your Marabanese was *that* good.'

He smiled. 'It isn't. But, like I said, Khalim taught me a few…*key*…phrases.'

Lara's heart began to pound. 'Like what?'

He felt her move away from him, and he missed her warm, sticky heat. 'Oh, just the kind of command to ensure a certain degree of…privacy. You know.'

Yes, she knew…or rather she was beginning to get the idea. Royal men took lovers, and for that they would not want a retinue of servants hanging around in the wings. But it was more than just privacy, she realised. For hadn't Darian just demonstrated in the most efficient way possible just how much he had been accepted into the royal fold?

What else had he discussed with Khalim, apart from how to ensure you could make love to a woman undisturbed? And that was the difference between the two men—Khalim would confide in Rose, but Darian would not do the same with her. Why would he? They were barely more than lovers, and even that was a tenuous link—one which would be broken once they had left Maraban.

Lara reached out for her jodhpurs, and the pair of panties

which were still rumpled up inside them, biting her lip as she thought how compliant she always was around him.

'Stop frowning, Lara,' he urged gently. 'Get dressed and we'll go back to our room.'

Her senses leapt in response to what he obviously had in mind, but she was troubled, too.

She had fallen for Darian big-time, but she had no idea where it was leading.

Or maybe she did. Maybe it was *that* which troubled her. For this thing between them—whatever it was—wasn't leading anywhere other than to the inevitable road to heartbreak.

## CHAPTER THIRTEEN

BACK in their room, Darian turned to her and smiled. 'I feel pretty hot and dusty,' he murmured. 'And that bath is big enough for both of us. Shall we take a bath together, Lara?'

She must snap out of it. They were lovers again, and hadn't she been wanting that to happen? What did she expect—that because they had just shared a delicious and erotic encounter in the stables that he would start offering her the moon and the stars?

She stretched, and yawned. 'Go and run it, then.'

'Or shall I have one of the servants do it?' he teased.

'Careful, Darian,' she said steadily. 'Much more of this and you'll come back down to earth with a bump when you get back to England!'

He didn't answer, just went into the bathroom and filled the tub with hot, soapy bubbles, and when he called her to tell her that it was ready she was already naked, and when he saw her his heart missed a beat. Their short and tumultuous history had not embraced any of the *normal* stuff, he realised. This was the first time he had seen her completely naked.

'You are very beautiful,' he said evenly.

But as his golden eyes slid over her Lara felt a little like one of the Akhal-Teke horses, being appraised for her physical attributes alone. 'Thank you.'

He pulled her into his arms, feeling her tension dissolve as he ran his fingertips up and down the smooth, satin flesh. 'Get into the bath,' he said huskily. 'You're shivering.'

The warm, silken water lapped over her skin, and she sank deep into it, watching while he stripped off his shirt and his jodhpurs until he was as naked as a gleaming, golden statue.

'Move over,' he instructed, and then his eyes became smoky and he smiled, his voice softening to a whisper. 'Actually, don't. Stay just where you are.'

Lara had never made love in a bath before and it was another out-of-world experience—the water providing weightlessness and making their kisses slippery wet, their limbs sliding and entwining and mingling until the obliteration of orgasm left her reeling and empty.

The water was cool by the time she opened her eyes, to find him looking at her.

'We'd better get out,' he said.

She nodded, but drew a deep breath, knowing that unless the subject were broached it would always be like an unspoken barrier between them. 'Darian, have you…have you forgiven me?'

'For?'

'For keeping secrets. And one in particular.'

His eyes narrowed. Why bring that up again, and especially now? 'It's forgotten.'

'Seriously?'

He shrugged his broad, gleaming shoulders, and tiny droplets of water ran down the tawny skin. 'I understand why you did it, okay?'

'That isn't the same as forgiveness.'

'Hell, Lara—can't you just leave it alone?'

'No, I can't!' With an effort she disentangled herself and climbed out of the bath—because somehow this needed to be said when she wasn't touching him, because touching distracted them both and detracted from the importance of what she was saying. 'I need you to know that when I said sorry I really meant it.'

He sighed as he followed her out and let the water go, hearing it gurgling and sucking away. Her words had the unmistakable ring of truth and regret, and they chipped away at his resolve. It was easier to think of her as foxy and deceptive, rather than soft and giving and warm and regretful. Qualities like that made him forget that this was something not dissimilar to a holiday romance. Two attractive people thrown together in a beautiful place, giving in to the pleasures of the senses without any of the hassle of normal day-to-day living.

'Forgiven and forgotten,' he said, and took her into his arms. 'Now, smile for me.' He dropped a kiss onto her trembling lips. 'That's better. Mmm. That's much better. Let's go to bed.'

'Now?'

'Sure—why not? Dinner isn't for hours.'

His body was close. Close and warm and overwhelming. 'That wasn't what I meant,' she said weakly.

He pushed himself even closer. 'I know it wasn't. But, in answer to your unspoken and rather sweet question, the answer is yes, I want to go to bed and make love to you. Again. But if you're tired…? He tilted her chin upwards, dazzled by the lost, dazed look in her blue eyes.

Tired? She had never felt more awake nor more on fire in her life. She stared into his face. The tawny hue of his skin was shadowed by the sculpted cheekbones and the faint darkening around his jaw. His lips parted a fraction and she touched her fingertip to them, tracing a line around them, biting back a wistful sigh. She wished that the doors of the palace could be boarded up and the two of them locked in here for ever, because she recognised that she had fallen in love with him, without rhyme or reason, nor even the comfort of having known him first as a friend.

She lowered her lashes, afraid that he might be able to read the emotion in her eyes, terrified that it would send him running—as surely it would. 'No, I'm not tired,' she murmured.

He gave a low laugh of delight, loving the way she gave him that demure little look even while the tension which was shivering over her body told him that she was feeling anything but demure.

He reached out and untied the knot of the belt at her waist, so that the robe fell open. He slid his hand inside, to cup her breast, its sinful weight resting in the palm of his hand, and felt the swift spasm of desire so strong and so intense that it was close to pain.

He was almost beyond words. Again. He shook his head, as if doing that would make clear some of the confusion making it spin. One touch and he was lost—or was that simply because he had been fighting her since they had arrived in Maraban? Surely it was just his appetite made keener by deprivation, rather than some dark, erotic power exerted by Lara, who could switch from wanton to demure and then back again?

'Come on,' he said huskily. 'Let's lie down before I fall down.'

'Not again! You really *are* a fallen man, aren't you?' she teased, because somehow it was easier to keep it light than to struggle with the enormity of how her feelings for him had just crept up and changed irrevocably. She wound her arms around his neck and looked up at him.

'I'll show you just how much, shall I?' he questioned softly, and picked her up and carried her through to the bed.

They slid between the Egyptian cotton sheets and he ran his fingertips lightly over her.

'Do you realise we're in bed properly together, at last? No sofas, no stables and no baths.' He gave her a look of mocking query. 'Isn't this how *most* people tend to do it, Lara?'

She doubted it. That was her last sane thought as he moved his hand between her legs. Surely it couldn't feel this good for other people? Surely they had just invented something new—just him and her? And could it just get better and better, like this? she asked herself afterwards in disbelief, as wave after wave of pleasure racked through her body once more.

Don't analyse; enjoy. Pretend it's a dream from which you'll never waken.

From that day on it felt like a honeymoon—without the declared love and the wedding, of course, but the days had about them a dreamy and blissful quality which was how she had always imagined a honeymoon to be. No worries and no reality. Lazy mornings and long, beautiful nights. And if Lara was acutely aware that it couldn't last for ever, that the sands of time were running out for what was only ever intended to be a short stay, she didn't confront it. Sometimes it was easier to hide from reality than have to face it.

Darian was no longer up at the crack of dawn to go to the stables, but Khalim still took them both out riding straight after breakfast each morning. Darian improved day by day—he was like a sponge, soaking up every single thing that Khalim told him and then fearlessly putting it into action.

'He will beat me yet,' Khalim sighed to Lara the first time Darian galloped, giving an exultant little whoop as he did so, and looking more carefree than she had ever seen him.

She nodded. 'Probably.' But he has me beaten already, she thought. Certainly my resolve not to fall in love with him.

'You are in love with him?' probed Khalim quietly, uncannily seeming to echo her thoughts. But then, he was a very perceptive man. He watched and he observed and he allowed instinct to guide him.

'Khalim!' She turned to him, knowing that her cheeks had grown pink. 'You can't possibly ask me a question like that.'

'I can ask anything I like—for I am the Sheikh!' he teased, but then his eyes unexpectedly softened. 'I think that you are, Lara. It is there for all to read when you are watching him and he cannot see you.'

'And Darian?' she questioned, her heart pounding, afraid of what she might hear. 'What do you see when he watches me?'

'I see a wary man,' said Khalim truthfully. 'He looks at you as I would a spirited horse who was perplexing me!'

Which was an ironic comparison when she stopped to think about it. 'Did he…did he say anything to you of what went on between us…before we arrived here?'

Khalim shook his head. 'He is a man who keeps his own counsel. He told me nothing, though some of it I have guessed.' He smiled. 'Do not worry yourself, Lara—these things have a habit of working out in the way that fate intends them to. Give it time.'

But it was borrowed time, and she did not know how long it would last. How long before this suspended state would be broken into by the demands of real living?

And then her question was answered. She saw the end in sight and a slow, waking dread came to life inside her.

They were waiting in the dining room when Khalim swept in. Only for once he did not dismiss the retinue which always accompanied him. His face was unusually stern, and Lara saw Darian's eyes narrow, as if he sensed that something was wrong.

'I must go to Dar-gar,' Khalim said immediately.

'Is it Rose?' questioned Lara at once. 'Is the baby all right?'

Khalim shook his head. 'Rose is fine and so is the baby,' he said gently. 'Though I have been away from her too long. No, my police have brought me news of a divisive element which is growing within the city walls, and my place is there.' He turned to Darian. 'You will accompany me?'

'Of course.'

Darian had agreed without hesitation, without even thinking about it for a moment, thought Lara sadly. But her sadness was for what might have been—for shouldn't she be joyful that Darian had a place here, that Khalim needed him, wanted him beside him to face the adversities as well as enjoy the pleasures of being ruler?

Darian had changed, even in the short time they had been here. It was perfectly plain to see if you looked properly—though maybe up until this moment she hadn't wanted to, or dared to.

Here in Maraban his presence seemed even more dominating than it had the first time she had seen him. He exuded an indefinable air that was much more than the power he had attained through his own successful career as a businessman. It was something which went deeper than that, and it was all to do with his royal blood. She had thought it when she had met him, and it was even more evident now. Maraban had released something in him, and in so doing it had bound him to the place for ever.

Darian belonged here, Lara recognised with a sinking heart. He did not need to wear the flowing robes of Khalim for anyone to be able to tell that at heart he was a true sheikh.

She had seen him discover a part of himself here which had been missing before. The golden eyes had become even more alive. She had watched the way they looked up at the clear Maraban sky every morning, watched him suck in a breath of pure, clean air and smile the smile of a contented man.

She had listened to the way he devoured facts about the country from Khalim, asking him this and asking him that, nodding his head as he absorbed as much of its history as was possible. Even the food they were served and the different drinks—he tried each and every one, and savoured them with the air of someone who had never really tasted before.

Last night, in bed, she had dared broach the subject of what might have been.

'Does it hurt?' she'd said softly. 'Or make you angry to think your mother had to struggle to survive when all this wealth was here for the taking?'

There was silence, so that for a moment she wondered whether or not he had heard her. Or overstepped the mark, perhaps, by trying to delve into his innermost thoughts.

Darian stared at the ceiling. He had been thinking about it a great deal, knowing that he had to come to terms with certain things or he would be unable to move on. If circumstances had decreed it, then he would have led a very different life.

'The question is whether or not Makim knew that she was pregnant,' he said slowly. 'Whether he refused to stand by her—*that* would make a difference to the way I felt.'

She stroked at his temple. 'And is there no way of finding out?'

'Oh, yes. He kept diaries. Khalim told me.'

'So read them! Find out.'

'There's a fifty-year rule about opening them,' he said slowly. 'Or at least it's fifty years before they can be brought into the public domain.'

So he would never know, or at least not until he was an old man, when the knowledge would no longer matter as much as it mattered now. 'Oh, Darian,' she said softly, and kissed his cheek.

Sometimes she was so damned soft and tender that he felt as weak as water, and Darian liked to feel strong. He turned over onto his elbow and concentrated on her pink and white naked body instead. 'Oh, Darian—what?' he questioned sulkily.

She remembered thinking fleetingly that he always put barriers up—that he went only so far before the shutters came down. But then he had made love to her in a way which made her misgivings melt away with the sureness of his touch, and afterwards she had cried softly, and she wasn't quite sure why.

She stood watching now as he talked to Khalim, their heads bent and deep in low conversation, excluding her completely.

'Lara, I will have the jet prepared for you,' said Khalim, straightening up.

She looked directly into the golden eyes which were trained on her watchfully. Make it easy for him, thought Lara. No bitterness, nor regrets, no tears or recriminations. Let it be a fond memory, something to warm him during the long, cold Maraban nights, until he finds another woman to replace me.

She nodded. 'I shall leave as soon as possible,' she said.

'How soon is soon?' demanded Darian.

Khalim glanced at his watch. 'You can be airborne within the hour.'

That quickly? Her head swam. But wasn't anything possible for the Sheikh of Maraban? That didn't even leave them time for one last, loving goodbye.

'I'll go and pack,' she said, noticing that Darian didn't attempt to change her mind for her.

She went back to their room, looking sadly at the rumpled sheets, which would normally have been changed while they were at dinner so that they would return to a neat and pristine bed for another night of long lovemaking.

It wasn't enough, she thought sadly. It had been too brief and all too beautiful, and then snatched away by chance and circumstance.

The door opened and her expression of regret quickly changed to one of acceptance. She would not burden him with her sadness, nor leave him remembering her face all crestfallen. And maybe in a way this was for the best. Ending naturally at its height rather than leaving her with a sour taste when it faded away, or he tired of her.

But inside her heart was breaking into a million pieces.

She clipped the suitcase closed and smiled. 'There!'

Darian looked at the tumble of dark, silken curls, the brittle way she was smiling at him. Something had changed. He knew it and she knew it, too. Yet wasn't it human nature to want things to stay exactly as they were?

'I don't want you to go, Lara.'

But Lara recognised that his words were inadequate, spoken only because it was the 'right' thing to say at a time like this. She shook her head. 'You need me to go, Darian. There is stuff here for you to do, and my presence isn't helping.'

'Yes.' There was silence for a moment, and when he spoke his voice was heavy. 'You know, I can't promise you anything, Lara. Not even whether or not I'll see you again.'

'I know that.' Her eyes were very bright, but her voice was steady. 'And neither should you. This has all been a very strange experience—perhaps it's best that we put it down to just that…an experience.'

She was moving away from him, and unexpectedly he felt a wrench. He reached out his arms to her, but she shook her head and turned away. If he touched her she would dissolve with the tears which were threatening to fill her eyes—and why leave him with *that* as an enduring vision?

'I'd better get going,' she said brightly. 'Can't keep Khalim waiting, can we?'

But he kissed her on the airfield, in full view of Khalim and servants and flight attendants and all. He brought his lips down on hers in a hard, almost punishing kiss, as if he wanted to physically imprint himself on her and leave her with a memory of him which no one else would ever be able to match.

But he hadn't needed to kiss her to do that.

## CHAPTER FOURTEEN

THE first thing Lara saw on her return to England was her face—only for a moment she didn't quite recognise it, for it was magnified to sixty-eight times its normal size, the blue eyes staring moodily down at her from a giant hoarding as her taxi drove out of Heathrow.

For a minute she blinked, disconcerted.

She had forgotten all about the job—the means she had used to get to Darian in the first place, which had ended up, ironically, with her winning the contract.

It was strange to see your features so enlarged. She looked all eyes—their sapphire-blue colour blinding—but there was a haunted, almost distracted quality to her smile, and she knew why.

It was the very first shot, and it had been taken just after he had put the shawl around her shoulders, when she had been disarmed by the soft and solicitous gesture. She was wearing the chiffon dress and holding the phone to her ear, and there was a dazed, almost dreamy expression on her face. It looked like the expression of a woman in love, but that was crazy. You couldn't fall in love that quickly could you?

She supposed that depended on what your definition of love was. Maybe she should settle for having been blown away by the man—a feeling which had subsequently grown. Now she was back in England and he was over in Maraban she was missing him already.

'That ain't you, is it?' asked the taxi driver, cocking his

head at the poster and then turning slightly to snatch a glance at her.

'Yes, it is.'

'Cor! Nice work if you can get it!' he enthused, and he screwed his nose up. 'Pay much, does it?'

It paid well, though not half as well as most people imagined. But in the end she had been the one who paid, and she had paid with her heart.

There was a light on in the apartment when she arrived home, and she didn't even have the energy or the inclination to fish around in her bag for her keys, just jammed her thumb on the bell and kept it there.

'What the bloody hell....?' An irate Jake flung the door open, his face immediately dissolving into an expression of concern when he saw her. 'Lara!' he exclaimed softly. 'Darling, are you all right? What in heaven's name has happened to you?'

'Oh, Jake!' And she dropped her bag onto the floor and collapsed, sobbing, into his arms.

It wasn't until she was settled on the sofa, a fire lit and a huge mug of steaming tea beside her, along with the remains of a box of tissues, that she felt ready to face his anxious questions. But the whole set-up sounded mad—in fact, it *was* mad—and nobody had told her what to say. Or what not to say. It was Darian's secret to tell. His story, not hers. And Jake was a darling, but what if he happened to let it slip to someone? She knew what the outcome of *that* would be. The press would have an absolute field-day, and Darian and Khalim's lives would be made hell.

'It's a broken heart, Jake,' she said. 'It's that simple.'

Jake was shaking his head. 'And it's that Darian Wildman who broke it? The one who, I hasten to add, was so foul-tempered to me! Want me to punch him for you, darling?'

Lara almost choked on her tea and laughed; it was a

relief to find that she still could. *'You?'* she questioned, with more emphasis than she had intended. 'Punch Darian? I don't think so, but thank you all the same!'

'I'll have you know that I came top in boxing in my year at drama school!' The famous blue eyes crinkled at the corners. 'But it's good to see you smiling. Now, sit there and put your feet up. I'm going to make us some supper.'

'Jake, you'd make someone a wonderful wife,' she sighed.

He turned round and raised his brows and for a moment looked so…so *imperious* that Lara suddenly got a good idea why he always featured in the 'Top Ten Most Wanted Men' lists which were periodically featured in newspapers and magazines.

'Don't push it, Lara!' he warned.

It felt weird to be back in England.

She tried rationalising it—telling herself that she had been in Maraban hardly any time at all, and certainly not as long as the time she had gone on a safari in Africa and ended up staying three months.

But comparisons didn't work. Maraban *wasn't* like anywhere else—its magic and its differences touched a part of her in a way that no other place did. And anyway, it wasn't the country she was yearning for. It was the man she had left behind there.

She forced herself to take a shower, even though she was reluctant to wash away the scent of him which still clung to her skin. That night her bed felt cold and empty, but not nearly so much as her body did. Strange how you could become used to someone. How quickly she had accommodated Darian's physical presence—and how badly she missed the warmth of him, holding her in the night.

The night wore on, the clock ticking away with a vengeance, as if calling time on her affair, and she told herself for the last time she would allow herself to cry, the tears sliding wet and warm down her cheeks and falling on the pillow.

In a way, it might have been better if it *had* been finished when she had left—at least then she might be able to mourn it properly and put a sense of closure on it. But it had been left unsatisfactorily open.

What had he said? *I can't promise you anything, Lara.*

It was hard not to try to read stuff into that—but if a girlfriend had told *her* a man had said that to her then how would Lara interpret it? As a courteous way of telling her there was no future in it?

*Not even whether or not I'll see you again.*

Definitely no future.

At least it didn't look as if there was going to be time to mope around the place, because the success of the poster campaign meant that work offers came flooding in. It was the highest public profile she had ever had, and suddenly it seemed that the world wanted to hire the tumble-haired brunette with the wide blue eyes.

Her professional life, it seemed, was on an all-time high, and she was impatient with herself for feeling that it was a very superficial kind of achievement. You worked all your life for something, and then when it came you couldn't appreciate it because you couldn't stop thinking about a wretched man!

She filmed a television commercial for a new brand of deodorant, and there were two magazine shoots lined up, as well as a whole diary full of 'go-sees'. And if she suddenly found the work curiously hollow, then surely that was to do with the constant aching in her heart.

Time was a great healer, that was what all the relationship experts said, and it had to be true or they wouldn't say it. If she never heard from Darian again then at least she could tell herself that what she had known with him in Maraban had been perfect. Too perfect, really, but there was no point dwelling on that. If she allowed herself to remember the way he had made her feel then it didn't exactly make the future seem a very rosy prospect, for she couldn't imagine ever recapturing that with anyone else. But at least she had felt it—no matter how fleetingly. Many people lived their lives without even coming close to it.

She walked into the apartment one night to find Jake lying on the sofa. She hadn't seen him for days because he'd been in Scotland, filming a new romantic comedy which was a follow-up to his last record-breaking success, and her mouth broke into a smile of welcome.

'Jake! Oh, how lovely to see you!'

'Hello, darling!' He looked her up and down. 'What's with the weight-loss?'

'Have I?'

*'Have I?'* he mimicked. 'Lara, you've dropped at least one dress size.' He frowned. 'From which I must deduce that you haven't heard from the Wild-Man?'

'I don't know why you call him that!' she said lightly.

'Because it's his name—only with maybe a slightly more sinister emphasis!' He narrowed his eyes. 'So have you?'

'No.'

'And how long's it been?'

Superstitiously, she didn't want to say it—because if she acknowledged just how long it had been then it might force her to confront the fact that it really was over. 'Six weeks,' she admitted reluctantly.

'So that's it, then? It's over?'

'Yes, Jake—that's it! I don't think you need to be a relationship counsellor to work that out! Now, I'm just going to send my sister an e-mail, and then I'll…I'll cook you supper—how about that?'

He smiled. 'That's my girl—welcome back to reality, Lara!'

He could keep it, she thought moodily as she sat down at the desk.

At least the computer provided a kind of refuge; she could see the appeal of a life spent surfing in cyberspace. If you were staring at, and communicating with a screen, it meant that you could escape from the real world and all the cares and worries it generated.

She switched on, gazing out of the window while the computer chugged into life, at the bare branches of the trees which were sketched across the ice-blue beauty of the winter sky. Would it ever be spring again? She gave a wan smile as she clicked the mouse onto her inbox. It was time to stop dreaming and get real indeed.

Twelve messages. One from each of her sisters. One from her agent and one from a schoolfriend with whom she corresponded sporadically. The rest were junk—which seemed to arrive daily, no matter what. She scrolled down, ticking each little box to delete them, then she stopped. Her head spun and her mouth dried.

*Golden Palace?*

Her heart seemed to miss a beat, even though she told herself that it was probably a Chinese restaurant touting for new business. But a Chinese restaurant would hardly title its subject matter: *Akhal-Teke and other things.*

Would it?

She clicked onto it, and now her heart was pounding with excitement. A sense of relief and delight washed over her as she realised that it was from him. Darian had e-mailed her!

The message read:

*Khalim and I have just arrived back from several weeks in the Dahab desert.*

So that was why she hadn't heard from him!

*Where he foisted upon me the most spirited Akhal-Teke you could imagine and told me to break her in! I did—after much bruising—and inevitably my new nick-name as 'Fallen Man' has been confirmed. How's life in London? Darian.*

She read it over. And over. And over again. Her heart was bubbling with a kind of happiness that she was sure was inappropriate. It was only an e-mail, after all. But deep down she knew it was more than that. He had re-established contact. He was still in her life. She wasn't sure in just what capacity, but at least he was there.

Should she wait to reply?

Hell, no! She had waited six weeks to hear from him—why punish herself by doing something just to appear 'cool' when she didn't feel in the least bit like that? In fact, her cheeks were flushed with a crazy excitement.

Her fingers were trembling. Keep it short, she told her-self. And sweet.

*London seems crazy and crowded—*

And lonely of course…

*But maybe that's because I'm comparing it with Maraban, which seems a very long way away.*

And then, because she couldn't possibly write what she really wanted, which was When are you coming home?—

he might have decided that Maraban was his home now—or, Darian, I love you and I really miss you—because that would be wholly inappropriate and he probably didn't feel the same way, she signed it, simply. *Lara.*

'What's up?' asked Jake, when she walked back into the sitting room.

'He's written! E-mailed me!'

'Wild-Man, I take it?' he questioned wryly.

'Will you stop calling him that?'

'That's his name, isn't it?'

'Oh, Jake,' she sighed. 'I didn't know they had e-mail in Maraban.'

'But they've got an army and a navy and an airforce,' he answered seriously. 'Why wouldn't they? What did he say?'

'Oh, just that he's spent several weeks in the desert with Khalim, that's all.'

'As you do!' joked Jake.

But Lara felt happy for the first time since she'd arrived back, and she hummed a little tune underneath her breath as she began to prepare a stir-fry for herself and Jake.

She developed a sudden and passionate interest in her e-mail inbox, forcing herself to only check it twice a day—once in the morning and once in the evening—though the temptation to sit there online all day, staring hopefully at the screen in case his name should float up, was almost overwhelming.

She knew that people said an e-mail didn't carry the same kind of clout as a letter. A letter you had to sit down and think about while an e-mail was fast and instant. Though this was not quite true in her case, because she would sit there dreamily gazing into space while thinking up replies, searching for just the right note to strike, reading and re-reading every one in case the wrong interpretation could be made of an innocent sentence.

She kept it light, told him about her jobs and her life, and sent some amusing anecdotes about a bunch of female fans who had discovered where Jake lived and were laying seige to the house.

A rather stern reply bounced back.

*Are they bothering you?*
*Get the police to move them on if they show any sign of trouble.*

And on one rare and wonderful occasion they managed to be online at the same time and he told her that he had met Rose. She wrote:

*Was she angry that I'd been there without getting in touch?*

He replied:

*She seemed to understand, just as Khalim said she would. I like her very much.*
*She says to send you her love.*

She typed, *Send mine back,* and waited, but that was it.

E-mailing could be a frustrating form of communication, she was coming to realise. One of you had to break it off first, and she could have sat writing to him all day. It wasn't as good as seeing him in the flesh, but it was a damned sight better than nothing.

And, in a way, it was another way of getting to know him—by the written word. It was rewarding and it was sweet to discover that she could make him laugh with some of the things she wrote—as he did her.

Christmas came and went and there was no present or card—but then they didn't celebrate Christmas in Maraban, and she didn't want a token anything from him. There was only one thing she really wanted, and that was the man himself.

But he sent her a sweet e-mail on Christmas Eve, reminding her to leave a mince pie for Santa and a carrot for the reindeer, and Lara went off happily to her parents' farmhouse, sighing as she hung up her stocking, knowing exactly what—or who—she would love to find inside on the following morning, pleased to lose herself in the messy, noisy chaos of a family Christmas.

But as a frozen January slipped into an even icier February, the e-mails became less frequent and when they did come they usually began with an apology.

*Sorry I haven't written for so long, but Khalim has been inducting me into the way of State Ceremonies.*

Lara strove to reassure him.

*It doesn't matter. Honestly. It's just lovely to hear when you do have time.*

And then, one evening, Jake took her to task.

She had just trailed into the sitting room when he looked up from his film script and pulled a face.

'War just started, has it?' he questioned acidly. 'No, let me guess—you haven't heard from Lover-Boy!'

'Leave it, Jake.'

'No, Lara—I will not leave it. How long are you going to continue living in a half-world? Happy when he writes—which is hardly ever—and miserable as sin when he doesn't?'

'He's been busy with Khalim,' she said miserably.

'Busy being an international playboy, probably,' said Jake darkly. 'It beats me why Khalim seems to have taken such a shine to him.'

And she couldn't tell him. She couldn't. She shrugged instead. 'I love him, Jake,' she said simply.

'Well, it doesn't look like he loves you back,' said Jake brutally. 'Better get used to it.'

Lara turned away, biting her lip and willing away the tears which were making her eyes swim. But deep down she knew he was right. She wasn't living, not really, or if she was it was in a fantasy world, just waiting for him to e-mail or recalling things he had said, things he had done—reading far too much into a remembered gesture or word.

Nothing had changed. He hadn't promised her anything then and he still hadn't, only now distance seemed to be asserting its natural power. The e-mails were fading away, and so, probably, were his memories of her.

Better join the real world again, Lara, she told herself.

That was what she did. She went to parties with Jake and fixed a bright smile of determined enjoyment on her face.

'That's my girl,' he murmured fondly. 'Pretend you're happy and one of these days you'll turn around and find that you actually are.'

She had to trust him on that one.

She needed a break, and a heavensent opportunity came in the shape of a weekend visit to her parents' farmhouse. It was their wedding anniversary and they were having a family party to celebrate. Lara hadn't been down since Christmas, and she was looking forward to seeing all her nephews and nieces. At least they wouldn't ask questions she would rather not answer about Darian—simply because she hadn't told them anything about him.

It was easier that way.

It began to snow as she left London, and the weather deteriorated still further on the way down, with great flurries of white flakes falling down endlessly from a gunmetal-grey sky. By the time she arrived she was frozen.

Her mother opened the door to her, looking anxious. 'Thank heavens you're here!' she exclaimed as an icy wind blew swirling snowflakes all around the hall. 'Come in and sit by the fire!' Then she frowned. 'And then, my girl, you are going to get some food inside you!'

Why did people keep trying to feed her up? Didn't they realise that food wouldn't fill the aching emptiness inside? 'Lovely,' she said obediently.

They had just finished a blow-out roast lunch and the noise levels had reached crescendo point. The table was a mass of crumpled napkins and half-eaten pudding, and one of her brothers-in-law was passing around some port which nobody really needed. Lara had her nephew sitting chubbily on her lap, attempting to build a little plastic aeroplane, when Lara's father frowned at his wife.

'Did you hear something outside?'

She smiled, fingering the gold necklace he had bought her like a newlywed. 'No, dear!'

'Maybe it's the lorry the necklace probably fell off the back of!' hiccuped the brother-in-law who had drunk the most port.

'Will you please shut-*up*, Jeremy?' demanded his wife.

The front doorbell chimed loudly and Lara's father frowned again.

'Not expecting anyone, are you, darling?'

Lara's mother shook her head. 'Today? And in *this* weather? Of course not.'

There was a pause, and Lara was filled with the strangest, giddiest sense of expectation.

'Better go and answer it, hadn't you?' she said, her heart beating so fast that her words sounded strangled.

Both her sisters turned and looked at her, both sets of eyebrows raised in identical sisterly question.

Even the children were silent.

They heard the door open and the sound of Lara's father speaking to someone, then a low, murmured reply. Ten expectant faces were turned towards the door of the dining room, listening as two pairs of footsteps approached.

'Wassamatter, Arnie La-La?' demanded her nephew, and Lara realised that she was gripping onto him very tightly indeed, instinct and a deep sense of hope and longing telling her who the caller might be.

She wanted it to be...but surely it couldn't...it just couldn't...

The world stood still and her heart clenched tightly in her chest as she stared straight up into a pair of rueful golden eyes, vaguely aware of her sisters both sitting bolt upright, making twin sounds of disbelief.

Well, she felt a bit like that herself—he looked so gorgeous. Strong and tall and lean as he stood there, just looking at her. She could scarcely think straight and her hands felt clammy.

'Darian,' she breathed.

'Hello, Lara,' said Darian softly.

# CHAPTER FIFTEEN

THERE was another pin-drop silence, and Lara wasn't surprised—because the sight of Darian standing in her parents' beautiful old farmhouse was slightly surreal—as if they had all been taking part in a black and white film and somebody had just stepped in in full Technicolor.

He wore jeans, and beneath a battered leather jacket was a warm, soft sweater, just like the one he had been wearing the first time she'd seen him. His hair was all ruffled, and sprinkled with snowflakes, and his skin looked even more vibrant and glowing than usual, his eyes shining with health and vitality.

Lara's mother coughed. 'Er, aren't you going to introduce us, Lara?'

'Yes, do, Lara,' said Heather, her oldest sister, in a voice which couldn't disguise her restrained excitement.

'This is Darian Wildman,' said Lara breathlessly. 'He's a…he's a friend of mine.'

The golden eyes gleamed in silent challenge.

'Won't you sit down, Darian?' said Lara's mother mildly, as if men who looked like Hollywood film stars suddenly appeared in her dining room every day of the week. 'And have some tea? Or I could probably rustle you up some lunch if you haven't already eaten.'

He smiled at her, and Lara watched her mother melt. 'I'd like that very much, Mrs. Black, but I wonder if first I could have a few words with Lara? In private?'

'Of course.' She looked at her daughter. 'Lara?'

Lara rose to her feet on legs which felt as if they had

suddenly been transformed into jelly. 'Let's go into the sitting room,' she said unsteadily.

The fire was blazing and there was a photo album lying open on one of the sofas. An empty champagne bottle was upended in the bin and there was crumpled wrapping paper from the anniversary presents lying waiting to be hurled on the fire. It looked messy and warm and homely.

Outside the window, the scene was startlingly white and beautiful, and Darian released a slow sigh as he turned to look at Lara properly, dressed in palest cream, her hair all loose around her shoulders, looking like a winter wonder herself. 'Lara,' he said softly.

Her heart was beating very fast. 'How the hell did you find me?'

'Jake told me where you were.'

'He *did*?'

'Eventually.' It had been like trying to extract blood from a stone, Darian remembered with a kind of grim admiration. 'He didn't want to. Gave me a great long lecture on how wonderful you were and how he wasn't going to stand by and see you hurt—but in the end I asked him whether you would be happier to see me than not, and then he told me where you were.' His eyes were very clear—clear and golden. 'So are you, Lara? Happy to see me?'

'I'm not sure how I feel,' she answered truthfully, because she didn't yet know why it was he had come.

He looked at the way her dark lashes were half lowered. 'You look very beautiful,' he observed softly.

'Thank you.' She let the lashes flutter up, cautious and wary. She felt as if she was skating on ice, without knowing how thin it was.

'But you've lost weight!' he accused softly.

She ran her eyes over the shadows and angles of his gorgeous face. 'Well, so have you!'

'I've been in the saddle every morning, riding through inaccessible parts of Maraban—what's your excuse?'

She didn't answer that. She didn't have to. She wasn't going to tell him that she had missed him and been pining for him, because that way she risked too much. Too much hurt if he told her, as she suspected he was about to, that he was going to stay in Maraban. That his life was there.

But if that was the case…

'Why are you here, Darian?'

'Can't you guess?'

Oh, but guessing was a dangerous game. She knew what she hoped, but she dared not risk saying it. What if her dreams were way off mark? Would that not just put him in the awful position—for him and for her—of having to reject her? But he's here, a little voice reminded her. He is *here.* 'I'm not a mind-reader.'

'Aren't you?' The last time he had made love to her he had thought she could see into his very soul. And he hers. God, it seemed like a lifetime ago now, and in a way maybe it was. 'Come over here, Lara,' he said, in a low, soft voice. 'You're a long way away from me.'

It was only a few steps, but it felt like a million, and Lara's feet took her slowly towards him like a child learning to walk for the first time. That was exactly how she felt. Unsure and uncertain and a tiny bit afraid.

He put his hand up and touched her cheek, saw her eyelashes briefly flutter down to shield her eyes, and when she opened them again they were bright. And wary.

'Why have you come here?' she whispered again.

'Because…' He searched for the right words, and wondered why they were so hard to find. Maybe because he wasn't used to saying what was really on his mind. And in his heart. 'I've…missed you.'

'Have you?' Her heart leapt in her chest. It wasn't the biggest declaration in the world, but maybe because of that it felt more real, more solid. For Darian was not a man to use words he did not mean.

He nodded. *Tell her how much.* 'Very much.'

It had been an entirely new sensation, one that he had tried at first to deny and then to rationalise his way out of—until he had realised that there *was* no way out, that for the first time in his adult life there was no template to follow. This was all very new to him, and exciting, and kind of scary.

His eyes gleamed very gold. 'Actually—very, very much.'

She could tell that he was choosing his words carefully, and the flicker of hope became a little steadier. 'Well, I've missed you, too.'

'Have you, now?' He smiled, but he saw how huge her eyes seemed in her face. She looked all wary, on edge. Fragile, as if she might just crumple up or dissolve. He felt a fierce rush of protectiveness and it took him by surprise—but why should it have done, when he stopped to think about it? Hadn't he been exactly that during that chaste first night together in Maraban? 'Don't you think we ought to sit down?'

She was pleased to, because her legs were feeling as wobbly as her emotions. They sat, side by side on the sofa, to the left of the roaring blaze, and while part of her longed for him to take her into his arms and kiss her the other part of her was enjoying his almost Victorian restraint. Passion was easy, but emotion wasn't. Not for Darian. Passion could be something to hide behind, and he wasn't attempting to.

She turned to him. His eyes looked different, she thought, as though he had seen something new—and maybe he had. 'So tell me about Maraban,' she said softly. 'What was it like in the desert?'

Darian's eyes narrowed. He realised that her focus was

absolutely right, though maybe that shouldn't have surprised him. Another woman might have wanted to talk about herself, about them, but Lara didn't. Had she sensed that his whole life and his whole perspective had changed? That change had somehow arisen out of the amazing experiences he had lived through, in the desert especially?

'It was just the two of us,' he began, his eyes narrowing with memory, taking him right back to the way it had been. 'Oh, there were guards stationed further down the mountain, of course, but in effect it was just me and Khalim. We rode, and we walked, and we talked. We did a lot of talking. We lit fires—it was *bloody* cold. The snows had set in, so we had to take food with us.'

'Not too much of it, judging by the look of you,' she said wryly.

'No.' He smiled. 'I guess it must almost have qualified as fasting.'

'And fasting is cleansing,' she observed, remembering the yoga course she had signed up for, until she had found sitting around saying 'Om' a bit boring and dropped out. 'Isn't it?'

'Very.' It had been the first time that he had ever really stopped, slowed down, really given himself time to think and to smell the roses. To look at his life and put it into some kind of perspective. 'Khalim offered me a place there,' he said slowly.

She had guessed that this might happen, had been mentally prepared for it, but even so it was still a shock. 'What kind of place?'

'To rule the western region of Maraban. To publicly acknowledge me as his brother—to legitimately make me…' He laughed. It sounded so bizarre—hell, it *was* bizarre—but that didn't mean it wasn't happening. 'Prince Darian of Maraban.'

Lara nodded. Heady stuff, being offered your own kingdom. Darian had influence and relative power in England, but nothing could compare to that. 'What did you say?'

He nodded slightly. She was perceptive indeed. She had not made any assumption about what his answer had been. 'I told him no.'

'My God,' she breathed. 'Was he angry?'

He shook his head. 'I think he was relieved, in a way. He made the offer out of filial loyalty, because he felt that it was right, and that only confirms what a remarkable man he is.'

'But why did you refuse it?'

For the first time he touched her. Picked up her hand and examined it, stroking the tip of his finger reflectively over the palm. It was both tender and yet curiously erotic, and Lara trembled. Was it still pretend tenderness, or was it real this time?

He felt her tremble and stopped stroking. Not yet, he thought. Not yet.

'I refused it because we are both strong men, and you cannot have two strong men governing side by side—it might work well as an ideal, but the reality of two such mighty egos clashing would be explosive!'

Yes, she could see that. 'But weren't you tempted?'

'By power?' he questioned slowly, and she nodded. 'For about a nano-second.' He looked very reflective for a moment, then gave a wry smile. 'But I could envisage the repercussions, should I accept such an offer. Maraban is Khalim's by birth as well as by blood. He knows his country more intimately than anyone. To bring in a man who is only half Marabanese would be to weaken the throne, supply subversive factions with a legitimate cause to revolt.'

'That's remarkably far-sighted of you,' she observed. 'Lesser men would have grasped at the chance of such power, no matter what the consequences, but not you.'

'No,' he agreed. 'Not me. Because lately I have learned too much to ever disregard what the consequences might be.'

There was a pause, and this time the silence had about it a quality which made Lara still, some instinct telling her that what he was about to say would be profound.

'And Khalim and I read his...*our*,' he amended, with a wry smile, 'father's diaries.'

Lara looked at him in astonishment. 'I thought you said there was a fifty-year rule preventing that?'

'So there is, but as Khalim rather arrogantly announced—why make the laws if you can't break them occasionally, too! Though they will still not be made public until the allotted time.' There was a pause. 'Makim knew nothing about my mother's pregnancy,' he told her quietly. 'That much was clear. He mentions her with great affection, but nothing more than that. It appears to have been a very passionate affair which had consequences of which he knew nothing.'

'And that makes a difference, doesn't it?' she questioned slowly. 'To you?'

He traced the line of her lips with the tip of her finger. 'Yes, it does. Of course it does.' He smiled. 'It means that I was not rejected nor forgotten by the Sheikh, nor denied a heritage that was truly mine. He simply didn't know anything about me.'

He tilted her face so that their eyes collided, blue with gold. 'But that's enough about Maraban.' His voice was soft now. 'I came here to talk about something quite different—something more important still.'

Her heart had begun to race. 'Oh?'

Once more he picked his words with care, recognising their significance and knowing how important it was that she believed them.

'I want to tell you why I came back,' he said simply.

'Oh?'

This was hard, to just come right out and say it, but he knew that he had to. For both their sakes. 'I never felt complete before, Lara.' He hesitated, trying to make sense of it. For her. And for him, too. 'Maybe that's the way it always is when you don't know what your true parentage is. And knowing is one thing, but seeing is something else. Seeing really *is* believing. When I tasted some of the life in Maraban, saw my father's home and land and the way he must have lived his life, I felt in a way as if I had come home.'

He paused, remembering how Khalim had told him that to feel deeply made you more of a man, not less. But it went against the grain with Darian. Old habits died hard. He had grown up believing that it was a sign of weakness to express your feelings. Yet now he recognised the importance of saying what he really meant, not hiding behind the tough, macho exterior which had been his childhood protection.

'When you discover your identity—you come home. You're at peace with yourself—at least in theory.'

She raised her face to his. 'I...I don't understand.'

It had taken him a little while, too. 'I found the peace which comes with knowing what my roots are, but I had lost something, too—the something that makes everything in life worthwhile. The something that makes living wonderful and the world an empty place if it isn't there.' He felt the thaw around a heart which had always been hard and tough and cold. It was like taking a leap into the unknown, he thought. Unexplored, uncharted territory—which took more courage to confront than any barren and inhospitable Maraban desert.

'Love, Lara,' he said simply. 'I found you, and I found love, and when you went away something was missing.

You'd struck a hammer-blow to my heart and it made me realise how much I wanted you in my life.'

'Oh, Darian,' she whispered, her voice faint, her blood pounding a symphony inside her head, weakened with pleasure and a sense of wonder. 'Darian.'

He smiled. 'But it wasn't the first time I'd felt that way.' His voice softened. 'I experienced it the first time I lay in your arms, but it scared the hell out of me. I put it down to the fact that we'd just had amazing sex. It made me feel vulnerable, you see, in a way I wasn't used to feeling. It's what made me not ring you.' He sucked in a deep breath. 'But I was blinding myself to the truth—then and later.'

'Oh?' The word was barely audible.

'That you were the missing part of the equation, Lara. That once you'd left Maraban it no longer felt like home. Home is where the heart is, and you have my heart. You were the factor which somehow made it all complete. Made *me* complete,' he finished, and it was a declaration so raw and intense that Lara felt rocked, shocked into a disbelieving silence.

'I love you, Lara,' he said simply. 'And I want you in my life. Permanently. Yours is the face I want to see first thing in the morning and last thing at night.'

Part of her was still scared that he was just saying it because he was in a heightened state of emotion, because all his past had coming flooding back in such a dramatic way. But when she looked into his eyes she saw the shining truth written there, and she knew she owed him nothing less in return.

'And I love you,' she said shakily. 'So very, very much.'

He touched her hair with a sense of wonder. 'When did it happen?' he mused. 'And how does it happen? In a moment? In a look, or in a kiss? In an emptiness when someone isn't there any more and you wish they were?'

'All of those things,' she agreed. 'And a few more besides.'

'Yes,' he said thoughtfully.

'Please, Darian,' she begged, 'will you just kiss me now?'

'Oh, God, Lara,' he said unsteadily. 'Try stopping me.'

He kissed her until he had to force himself to stop, drawing his lips away from her dazed and reluctant face.

'Oh!' She pouted. 'Why did you do that?'

He moved away with difficulty. 'I hardly think it will make a good impression on your father if he comes looking for us and finds the door to his sitting room locked! Come on,' he said tenderly. 'Let's go and find your family.'

Nothing more was said, not then, but nothing needed to be and nobody asked. Maybe it was plain for everyone to see, thought Lara. They went back into the dining room, where her mother had cleared the table and made tea, and Darian sat down and was welcomed and introduced properly.

She feasted her eyes on him as he solemnly began to assist her niece in dressing her new dolly while her smallest nephew tugged insistently at the leg of his trouser, and he looked up at her and smiled, and it was all there, written in that silent and loving curve of his lips.

It seemed nothing short of a miracle that the two of them had been brought together, to this sweet, satisfying conclusion. Fate, Khalim would have said. Predestination.

And she believed in it, too.

She didn't know what their future would bring—but then, who did? Life was a journey and so were relationships, and theirs had begun properly today.

I love you, Darian Wildman, her eyes told him, and silently his eyes told her he loved her back.

## EPILOGUE

EVERYONE in the village said there had never been an event like it, and they were quite right. The wedding of the youngest Black girl took place in a tiny village church in the middle of the English countryside and was attended by the leading members of the Maraban royal family!

'Won't people ask questions?' Lara had asked Darian anxiously one morning, when she was trying to get out of bed.

He pulled her back into his arms. 'Ask what?' he said, his voice muffled, but then it was very difficult to talk at the same time as you were kissing somebody's neck.

'About…' Lara closed her eyes. This was hopeless. She couldn't think straight—but then, in his arms she always felt like that. 'About why Khalim and Rose and the children will be there.'

'Rose is your friend,' he said simply. 'That's all anyone needs to know.'

For, after much thought and discussion with Rose and Khalim, they had decided to keep Darian's ancestry a secret. Nothing would be gained by him acknowledging a title which he had no intention of claiming, and neither of them wanted the intrusion that media interest would bring, nor the risk of Maraban dissidents knowing where they lived.

But Darian had fallen more than a little bit in love with the country, and his latest career direction had taken that fact into account. He was now establishing new trade links between Maraban and the West, becoming a sympathetic and enthusiastic advisor to Khalim, his brother.

Lara's family had welcomed him with open arms—he had won them over that first day, each and every one of them—and Lara's mother had taken her aside just before they'd left to go back to London.

'You're a lucky girl,' she had said wistfully. 'He loves you very much.'

She didn't need to be told that. Sometimes Lara felt that she had to pinch herself, to see whether it really could be true—but it was. And with love had come other changes. She had taken a new career path, discovering that she no longer wanted to chase bit parts in stupid commercials or play a minor character in a show which seemed to close almost as soon as it had opened. Nor put herself up for rejection every time she went on a 'go-see'. She felt she had been given so much that now she wanted to put something back.

Soon after she moved into Darian's apartment she had enrolled on a course to learn how to teach drama, and that was how she saw her working future. At least until the babies came. Lots and lots of them. She wanted that, and so did Darian. He would find them a house somewhere and they would build a home together, fill it with noise and warmth and, she hoped, children.

She wanted to give him what he had never had. What she had seen on his face that snowy winter day as he had embraced her little nephews and nieces—the joy of being part of a whole big family. He had found part of his family in Khalim and now it would just grow and grow.

Even Jake had come round to accepting him. The two men had gone out for a 'quick' drink one evening, and had rolled in at midnight, both rather tight. Lara had scolded them for not letting her know, bursting into laughter when she returned with a tray of strong coffee to find them both slumped together in companionable sleep.

In front of a video of one of *her* old plays!

It had taken a year before he had asked her to marry him. He had wanted to ask her that day at her parents', but had held off, recognising that they needed something of which they had had precious little.

Time.

But time was a funny thing. It only echoed what you were feeling inside. When you were waiting for a train an hour could seem like an eternity, and when you were sitting an exam that same hour could seem like a minute.

And so it had been with him and Lara. The first time he'd seen her something had touched him, only he had been too stubborn and pig-headed to acknowledge it. Theirs had not been a smooth and easy journey to get to where they were today, but maybe that was what made it so very good. You had to experience pain to appreciate pleasure, and the pleasure she gave him was immeasurable.

Darian turned his head as the organist began to play and Lara began to walk towards him, a vision in a sheath of slippery white satin, her arms full of snowdrops and lily-of-the-valley.

His eyes were on her the whole time, and when she reached him she gave him a loving smile. He smiled back, and the warmth inside his heart increased so that it felt as if he had a small furnace burning away inside him.

After a lifetime of resistance Darian was learning to articulate his feelings, but with Lara that was easy.

He had never known it could be so easy.